50 States of Fear
ALASKA

The Dork and the Deathray

E.G. FOLEY

Other Books by E.G. Foley:

The Haunted Plantation (50 States of Fear: Alabama)
Leader of the Pack (50 States of Fear: Colorado)
Bringing Home Bigfoot (50 States of Fear: Arkansas)

The Lost Heir (The Gryphon Chronicles, Book One)
Jake & The Giant (The Gryphon Chronicles, Book Two)
The Dark Portal (The Gryphon Chronicles, Book Three)
Jake & The Gingerbread Wars (A Gryphon Chronicles Christmas)
Rise of Allies (The Gryphon Chronicles, Book Four)

ALASKA

- ➤ Alaska – the 49th State!

- ➤ State Capital: Juneau

- ➤ State Motto: "North to the Future"

- ➤ Nickname: The Last Frontier

- ➤ State Flower: Forget-Me-Not

- ➤ State Bird: Willow Ptarmigan

- ➤ Top Family Attractions: Glass-domed train rides on the Alaska Railroad; Matanuska Glacier, accessible by car; Mount McKinley, the tallest peak in North America; dogsled rides (feel the speed and power); native wildlife watching (including moose) at Creamer's Field Migratory Waterfowl Refuge.

- ➤ Must Eat: Anything salmon (smoked, cured, jerky, sweetened into a candy)

- ➤ Weird Fact: Barrow, Alaska is the northernmost city in the United States. When the sun sets on November 19th, it won't rise again for about sixty days (polar night). Conversely, when the sun rises on May 12th, it won't set again for about eighty days (midnight sun phenomenon).

- ➤ Some Famous Alaskans:
  Sarah Palin – Alaska governor, vice presidential candidate
  Elizabeth Jean Peratrovich – Tlingit (Alaska natives) activist
  Bob Ross – Host of *The Joy of Painting* television show
  Jewel – Singer-songwriter, actress

Uncle Scram's Alaska Travel Tip:

You're not paranoid, they really ARE out to get you...

Table of Contents

Authors' Note

Bonus Chapter!

About the Authors

Prologue
Revenge of the Nerd

When your mom was an astrophysicist at NASA and your dad wrote code for the NSA—and when *you* were born with an IQ that could get you on the university chess team when other kids were still learning their ABCs—only one thing was certain. You were destined from birth to become a nerd of epic proportions.

By age thirteen, such was Kelvin Mackowsky's fate.

With his freakish intelligence, poor social skills, and a regrettable smattering of zits, he had already experienced more than his share of rejection in life.

Only now, he no longer cared. At least that's what he told himself.

Inspired by the pages of his comic book collection, he had recently decided how to handle the fact that he didn't fit in: by becoming the world's youngest supervillain.

Starting tonight.

Ah, then all the people who had refused to accept or even *try* to understand him...well, soon they'd be sorry.

Deviously clever as he was, Kelvin gave his CIA handlers no sign of his true intentions as the black helicopter they were riding in raced over endless miles of remote Alaskan forest.

A crackly voice radioed to warn them they were entering restricted military airspace well before the Northern Lights facility came into view. When the pilot gave the proper security codes and told the control tower they were bringing in the expected VIP, the tower granted clearance to approach the installation without fear of being shot out of the sky.

No need to scramble the fighter jets.

Of course, *he* was the VIP they meant. Kelvin the Wünderkind, who had been on the cover of *Wired* magazine last year just after his twelfth birthday with the headline: MEET THE DARLING OF DARPA.

(Which stood for Defense Advanced Research Projects Agency. Which meant they invented funky, cool, futuristic weapons systems and other fun things. Which, if someone told you about, they'd probably have to kill you.)

Kelvin sat forward in his seat as the Northern Lights compound came into view over the next forested ridge. It wasn't much, really—a big, dull, rectangular building surrounded by a barbed wire fence, surveillance cameras, and untold layers of security.

But a sly smile spread over his face as the most interesting part of the facility, the thing he'd come for, came into view. "Hello, beautiful," he murmured under his breath, staring at it.

Geek heaven!

It really was too bad he didn't have any friends his own age, he mused. While other boys dinked around with video games, he was about to play with one of the federal government's billion-dollar high-tech toys.

The conspiracy nuts called it "Tesla's Deathray," but that was oversimplifying things.

The Northern Lights array was so much more.

Behind the ominous fencing, several football fields' worth of ground were covered with row upon row of giant radio antennas. One transmitter, bigger than the rest, stood in the center.

There were hundreds of them in what was called a phased array, all wired together and aimed at the sky, ready to blast out an energy beam of massive power. Well, every supervillain had to start somewhere, and Kelvin had a theory about how certain frequencies could be used...

This is going to be fun.

His heart beat faster as the black helicopter finally touched down. Even before the blades stopped turning, Kelvin's handlers jumped out of the chopper.

Jailers was more like it. Muscle-neck John Barnes was ex-Special Forces, and the supermodel blonde was CIA, Agent Samantha Wilkes. Kelvin pitied the guys who tried to ask her out on dates.

As for him, it was not easy having those two as his round-the-clock nannies. They were not exactly the warm-and-fuzzy type. But at least they made sure that the North Koreans, the Russians, the Chinese, or any others didn't snatch America's famous (soon to be infamous!) MENSA-freak boy brainiac.

Kelvin tolerated the pair. He didn't have much choice.

Meanwhile, the high-security doors of the Northern Lights research building slid open and two of the staff scientists strode out to meet him and his bodyguards, white lab coats billowing in the breeze.

"Welcome to Northern Lights, Dr. Mackowsky," the first scientist greeted him. "I'm Dr. Beth Ambry, chief research coordinator. This is my colleague, Dr. Martin Figgs. Dr. Figgs is our most senior researcher. It's such an honor to have you with us."

"Yes, I'm sure it is. Call me K-Mack," he said, his voice cracking a little. He winced. It sort of killed the cool effect he was going for, but ah well. Even a supervillain had to go through puberty.

"Uh, Dr. K-Mack?" Dr. Figgs echoed.

Samantha rolled her eyes and shook her head at the scientist as if to say, *Ignore him. That's his new kick.*

Kelvin frowned when the gray-haired scientist eyed his outfit a little strangely. In truth, not even *he* was quite used to his new supervillain look. He felt reasonably cool in his black turtleneck, black leather jacket, and the small, rectangular, European-style glasses that he now wore instead of his old, round, dorky Harry Potters.

Though, to be sure, he, too, was a kind of boy wizard.

He snapped his black-gloved fingers and a huge, bald security guard went to get his duffel bag and laptop out of the chopper.

At once, he snatched his briefcase out of the man's big meat hooks.

Kelvin *always* carried his briefcase personally. He couldn't have that falling into the wrong hands; it held his research and his latest little devious inventions.

4

"How long will you be staying with us, er, K-Mack?"

"Oh, hard to say, Dr. Ambry," he drawled.

"Well, we have a nice suite ready for you in our living quarters. I think you'll be quite comfortable for the duration of your visit."

"Our rooms are next to his?" Samantha clipped out.

"One on each side, Agent Wilkes, just as the Company requested."

The Company, of course, meant the CIA.

Kelvin had been recruited as an asset a couple of years ago, whether he liked it or not, thanks to his genius parents' government connections.

They had offered him up with pride like a sacrifice to Uncle Sam.

Thanks a lot, Mom and Dad.

He was a chip off the old brainiac block, but a family of software engineers wasn't big on emotion.

Well, anyway, maybe he could've handled being a world-class nerd, but after several years of brooding, Kelvin had decided that he couldn't stand another day of living like the Company's coddled prisoner.

They said he was a hero for using his brains to serve his country, but he couldn't think of a single person out there in America who even cared about him or wanted to be his friend.

The CIA only wanted him for his inventions, and every time he created something new, he had nightmares, wondering how the overlords of DARPA would use it.

"If you'll all come this way," Dr. Ambry said with a polite gesture at the building.

They followed as she walked them toward the door, her high heels clicking on the cement path that led up to the entrance.

"We'll have to set up your biometrics so you can come and go as you please," she said.

"He's already got an RFID chip implanted in his ankle," Samantha offered helpfully.

Yep, Kelvin thought, clenching his teeth at the reminder. No chance of ever running away.

"Good!"

"There are lots of fun outdoor activities for you around here, Dr. K-Mack," Dr. Figgs offered. "That's what Alaska's all about. Can't be all work and no play for a boy your age, right?" He beamed a smile at him. "Think you might like to do some hiking? There's amazing rock climbing nearby, horseback riding, whitewater rafting..."

His voice trailed off as Kelvin stared at him. "Do I look like the outdoorsy type to you?"

Dr. Figgs pursed his lips, and then Dr. Ambry changed the subject, back to business. "Iris scan, handprints, voice profile. We use all three, considering the top-secret work we do here."

"Why, I thought you were just studying the aurora borealis," Kelvin said in a voice dripping with sarcasm.

Dr. Ambry laughed uneasily, obviously realizing her mistake.

Barnes leaned closer to her. "Gotta ask, then, since you brought it up... That hurricane that coldcocked Cuba last week— was that you guys?"

She smiled nervously at the warrior. "No, of course not!"

Sweat burst out on Dr. Figgs' forehead. "Gracious! I don't

know *what* you folks are talking about! We're just here to study the electromagnetic properties of the ionosphere. You know, so we can understand how to improve our global communications and so forth."

Kelvin was mildly amused with the whole charade. Barnes shrugged the matter off. But Kelvin gave the ancient doctor an approving wink without the others noticing. The old man knew better than anyone that Uncle Sam didn't spend a billion dollars to study how to improve communications.

That was just the cover story the government told the dumb workhorse taxpayers. Fortunately, the mainstream media repeated the lie enough times that everybody believed it.

Well, almost everybody.

There were those who had long ago figured out the truth, but they were easily dismissed as conspiracy kooks.

Nevertheless, very few of even them could have imagined what Kelvin had planned for the antenna array. It was going to be the greatest show on earth...

Ladies and gentleman! Children of all ages! For my next trick, I present to you an ordinary antenna field. Watch closely now, as I add one giant spoonful of ELF waves, a dash of midrange radio frequencies, and a great big unhealthy bundle of pulsed microwaves. I stir it all together and abracadabra, zip-a-dee-doo-dah, what do we get? A heaping blast of mind control, right in your face! And it's all bought and paid for by you.

Kelvin forced himself not to laugh out loud.

Once they were safely past all the layers of security, Dr. Ambry gave them a quick tour that ended in the thirteenth-floor control room.

Kelvin sauntered over to a bank of monitors, then stole a nonchalant glance over his shoulder at his security guard. The one that never ate, never slept, and most importantly, did everything Kelvin ordered.

While the perky Dr. Ambry rattled on, playing her part perfectly now, Kelvin reached into his pocket and pulled out a small black device. He started feverishly pressing its touchscreen. He looked like a kid trying to send a text in class without letting the teacher see.

Of course, he didn't have any friends to text with, and besides, the message he was sending was wirelessly delivered straight into the bodyguard's neural network.

The large, black-suited security officer suddenly squared his massive shoulders, lifted his jaw, and slowly turned toward his boss for orders.

Kelvin could barely contain his excitement.

The moment to carry out his Evil Plan had come.

With the press of a button and a supervillainous smile, he silently gave him the command: *Attack*.

Well programmed as he was, the bodyguard obeyed.

He had no other choice, really.

And once K-Mack the Awesome took control of Northern Lights, neither would anybody else.

Muahaha.

Chapter 1
My Ruined Summer

Even the inmates at Alcatraz had more freedom than I did that summer...

The summer of the riots.

The chaos started one day out of the blue with no explanation, like somebody flipped a switch, and the American public suddenly went nuts.

Ordinary people flooded out into the streets. Soccer moms started smashing store windows, looting shops in the mall. Businessmen began beating up innocent bystanders. I even saw little old ladies throwing bricks at the police, who answered with tear gas and curfews.

It was ugly, and the mayhem was spreading fast. New York, Atlanta, Cleveland, Philadelphia, Baltimore, Chicago, Dallas. Before long, the craziness broke out in other cities and even some small towns.

Mom said that people were getting desperate because the economy was so bad and the stock market tanked again.

Whatever.

All I knew was that I had somehow survived sixth grade only to find my long-awaited summer break ruined.

Of course, the riots also reached the West Coast. Maybe not so shocking that half of LA was on fire by late June. Kind of a given.

But even in my oh-so-civilized home city of San Francisco, I kept hearing fierce, high-tech, military helicopters buzzing low over our building nearly every day, shaking the whole apartment. I would run out to the balcony to look at them and marvel at their double sets of whirling blades, and I'd wave at the SWAT guys whooshing past overhead like tense superheroes on a mission.

But they were all business, on their way to stomp down the rampaging citizens, and not at all interested in waving back to one super bored girl.

So, it was Alcatraz for me.

Actually, I spent a lot of time staring at that sinister old prison out on its lonely island rock. I could see it through my binoculars from the balcony of our apartment. That was as close to being outside as I was allowed to go without an adult because of all the craziness out there.

I don't *like* being treated like a baby.

Oh well. At least our apartment had a good view of the beautiful San Francisco Bay. The seals were free, playing in the deep blue water, sunning on the rocks.

As for me, I was a little bitter. School was out, and we lived in a place with the best weather known to man, but I was stuck inside all day, every day. I wasn't allowed to ride my bike, practice my tumbles in the park, surf, take a jog on the beach. Nothing!

All through June and early July, as my mother rushed out the door to go to work, our conversation would go something like this:

"I'm going crazy, Mom. I'm so bored. I need some fun. I need to get out of here!"

"I'm sorry, Gabby, but violence can break out at any second. It's just not safe to go anywhere. Try to have some *indoor* fun. Do some crafts. Write a blog. Practice your gymnastics floor routine, your ballet."

"Ugh! Mom, it isn't healthy for a kid to be cooped up like this. I need some fresh air. I can't take it anymore!"

"Well, honey, I don't know what to tell you. Open the upstairs windows or something, because you're staying inside. End of discussion! Just try to keep busy while I'm at work, and we'll play some games when I get home tonight."

Then she would blow me a kiss, step outside, and slam the front door. Without fail, she would lock the deadbolt and jiggle the handle to make extra sure that her little prisoner was safely locked away for yet another day of solitary confinement.

Her parting words were always the same and always shouted through the door so I couldn't see her face to tell if she was lying or not. "Things will calm down soon, Gabby. You'll see."

Click, click, click... Her heels would fade away, out into the scary city.

She was worried, and as a spokesperson for the mayor's office, I knew perfectly well that she had inside information about what was really going on.

I got the feeling from all the things she *didn't* say that it was actually worse than what the reporters were telling on the news.

No wonder. The talking heads on TV didn't even pretend they were telling the truth. They just read whatever was on their preprogrammed teleprompters, designed to keep the people calm.

Not that it was working.

People were so angry. It was as though everybody was on edge but no one could quite tell you why.

Well, except for the Tinfoil Hat people. They certainly had a theory about things.

They cracked me up.

I'd been watching the super boring news one afternoon, expecting my mom to come on, as per usual, to make a comment from the mayor's office. It's amazing how she doesn't get nervous when she does those press conferences, taking questions on camera from the reporters.

Anyway...

That was when the first Tinfoil Hat guy I ever saw burst on camera, totally uninvited. The news-anchor lady had been standing there with a big plastic smile on, saying that the authorities had the situation under control, and suddenly, there he was.

"It's the aliens!" he yelled, a wild-eyed, disheveled nutcase, shoving her aside. "They're shooting beams at us from the skies, people!" He pointed to his head, which was wrapped in tinfoil. "Protect yourselves or they'll hack into your brain!"

I laughed hysterically at that.

"Sir! Excuse me!" the anchorwoman huffed in outrage, gesturing to someone offscreen.

"Don't listen to her, she's probably a cyborg!" yelled the nutcase. "The New World Order is here! They're lying to all of us—"

Somebody off camera abruptly rushed in and grabbed the poor fellow, dragging him away, while I sat there shaking my head in astonishment.

"Well!" I turned to my fat, lazy hamster, Napoleon, sitting in his cage nearby. "Aliens, huh? I feel so much better now. That explains everything."

Napoleon wasn't interested.

The outlandish man, however, had given me an inspiration to help ward off my boredom for yet another hour. I jumped up from the couch and ran into the kitchen, got out the tinfoil, and giggled as I formed it into a variety of very fashionable hat shapes.

Oh, I looked beautiful. At least, my hamster and my tank full of grumpy goldfish thought so.

They had been acting weird those days, too, come to think of it. My fish kept bumping into the sides of their tank as though they were confused, and every now and then, Napoleon would jump onto his wheel for no apparent reason and start scurrying furiously at top speed, like he had to provide electricity for the whole city by turning that wheel.

It had been very strange, but for now, he just sat there in his cage with a curious look on his little face while I took out my phone and snapped some cute pics of myself wearing this season's collection of tinfoil hats.

I tried to send them to my girlfriends, but once again, dang it, no cell service!

That was the worst part of everything. My friends and I couldn't even text each other like normal. It was *agony* being out of touch.

Yep, I guess that alien mother ship must have been shooting down some invisible beams at the cell towers, messing with the signals or something.

Little did I know at that point how close to the truth the Tinfoil Hat guy actually was.

Only, it wasn't aliens or the New World Order. It was just one bratty teenage boy with zits and self-control issues.

But don't let me get ahead of my story, because at that point, I had not yet met Kelvin the Evil Dork.

What actually happened next was this...

# # #

The landline rang on yet another beautiful sunny Saturday afternoon. I didn't feel like picking up. I was in, shall we say, a mood. Landline calls were always for Mom, anyway, and since she was home, *let her get it.*

I had *way* more important things to do. Like painting my fingernails for the third time that week. Neon purple this time. Three rings... Four rings...

"Mom!"

Five rings...

Mom wasn't picking up. *Fine, I'll get it.* I heaved a sigh, feeling extremely put-upon, and picked up the phone, managing not to smear my nails. "Hello?"

"Ouooowaaa!"

I frowned and looked at the receiver in confusion, then put my ear to it again cautiously. Crank call? "Uh, hello? Who's there?"

I heard some rustling sounds, followed by deep animal snorts and a few grunts.

What kind of weirdo...?

It sounded like a pig digging in the dirt. This was followed by another loud, bizarre bellow. "Ouooowaaa!"

All of a sudden, I realized it could only be one person. I rolled my eyes, smiling. "*Dad!* Is that you?"

More animal noises.

I have the coolest dad on the planet. A little crazy, but totally awesome. "Dad. I know it's you." I sat down, grinning. "Have you lost *your* mind, too?"

"It's a moose call, Gabby," he calmly informed me.

"Oh really?"

"Think of it as the call of the wild."

That's my dad for you, always goofing around. He would do just about anything to make me laugh. My parents are divorced, and so I only see him a couple of times a year. We talk on the phone when he's not traveling the world for work.

Dad makes wildlife documentaries. Awesome, huh? You've probably seen him on one of the science-and-nature channels. He's the tanned, blue-eyed guy with long blond hair that half the older ladies in the world are in love with.

Ugh. There's even a Chase Reynolds Fan Club with T-shirts and everything, but Dad can't be bothered with answering e-mails from all the middle-aged women who have crushes on him.

Chase Reynolds, adventurer with a camera, craves excitement and adventure. *Lives* for it. Though he is the poster boy for laid-back California cool, Mom is always quick to point out how hard it can be living with an adrenalin junkie.

Dad travels to all kinds of amazing locations filming beautiful places and getting too close to dangerous beasts, just to get the perfect shot.

Obviously, a guy like that doesn't do boredom well.

That must be where I get it from, because I'm known to my teachers at school as The Girl Who Can't Sit Still. Even sitting at my desk, I can't help doing small versions of my ballet stretches now and then or I'll start twitching.

"So, how was the Great Reef, Daddy?"

"Awe-inspiring, Spud."

"Meet any great whites?"

He just laughed. "Wait till you see the footage. That's all I'll say. More importantly, how are you doing? I hear it's crazy town up there."

"Uh yeah!" I said in exasperation, then I hung my head. "Oh, Dad, I'm bored out of my skull! Mom won't let me leave the apartment! My friends' moms won't let them come over, either. It's horrible, Dad. I'm in jail!"

"Not for much longer, kid," he responded.

I held my breath. "What do you mean?"

"How would you like to hang out with your old man for a week and a half? I'm thinking about laying some groundwork for my next project, spotting locations and meeting some contacts.

That sort of thing. Wanna tag along?"

"Really?" Instantly I longed to go, but then I groaned. "Mom will never go for it. She always thinks you're gonna get me killed."

"Nope, this was actually your mom's idea. She called me last night. She thinks now's a great time to get you out of the city and into the great outdoors for some fun."

I could hardly believe my ears. I felt like I was getting paroled early for good behavior. Honestly, I hadn't even been that good!

"So, what do you say?" he prompted.

"Dude, I'm so there!"

He started laughing. "Don't you want to know where we're going first? I'll give you a hint: We might run into some mooses. Meese. Mices?"

"Just moose, Dad." I knew he was only trying to make me laugh again, and it was working.

Frankly, it didn't matter where we were going. I was just so happy to finally be getting out of my house and spending some time with my surfer-dude, anything-goes dad.

But I could tell he was bursting to share the secret, so I humored him. "Okay, where are we going?"

"To the land of the midnight sun, Gabby," he said, putting on his Suspenseful Documentary Narrator voice. "A place where it's only dark for a few hours a night this time of year. Can you guess?"

"I think so," I said, grinning from ear to ear.

Now his voice was brimming with excitement. "It's gonna be gorgeous. It's gonna be mysterious. It's gonna be a rad adventure, so pack your shades, baby, we're going to Alaska!" he yelled.

I shrieked with happiness, then bounced into a handspring off the coffee table.

I could hear him laughing through the receiver where I had set it down. "Yo, Gabby! Are you still there?"

I picked it up again and told him in three words exactly what I thought of him. "Best. Dad. *Ever!*"

Chapter 2
The Great White North

Five days later I was in a hotel room in Anchorage, Alaska, a world away from all the craziness and riots.

We had been in town less than twenty-four hours and already I was in heaven. The scenery was breathtaking, the air was crisp and cool, and the city on the edge of the Last Frontier, as they call it, charmed us with its whole rustic vibe. Beyond the streets of Anchorage, magnificent nature beckoned from the horizon everywhere you looked.

It was great fun to watch my dad work, too. He was kind of obsessive, taking his preliminary photos, fussing over his equipment, hashing out his script, and setting up meetings with experts.

He's a great talker, though. He told me once that schmoozing the locals always gets him inside information. He can strike up a conversation with anyone, anywhere. That's probably why he's so likable on camera.

But his real passion is for the adventure, so he couldn't wait to get out into the mountains to find the best places for spotting wildlife. He has a really sharp eye for what looks good on film.

On the fourth morning of our trip, we had plans to take a helicopter down the coast. We would be spending the night at Glacier Bay National Park and then head back to Anchorage the following afternoon. Tons of video ops.

I have to admit, I was a little nervous about the helicopter ride, but I kept my fears to myself and quietly swallowed them down like yucky cough medicine.

I would never admit to being scared 'cause, after all, I'm Chase Reynolds's daughter and he's not afraid of anything. I didn't ever want him to think his daughter was a wimp.

Dad was packing his equipment while I was fiddling with the old-fashioned clock radio on the nightstand. I was having a hard time getting anything to tune in, so I switched to AM, and all of a sudden, a raspy voice boomed through our hotel room.

"Wake up, America, the New World Order is here! I'm RJ Hopper and I'm hoppin' mad! Excuse my rant, but I don't like seein' my country turned into a police state! You think all of these riots are happening by accident? You think everyone just woke up one morning and decided to lose their minds?"

"Hey, it's a Tinfoil Hat show," I told my dad with a grin.

"There's something going on in that facility up in Alaska, people!" the scratchy-voiced man on the radio continued. "They can lie about it all they want, but President Eisenhower warned this nation decades ago about the military industrial complex taking over and now they've got a deathray!"

"Whoa, cool, a deathray," I said.

"You better be takin' this seriously out there! My inside

sources have risked their lives to bring me this information, so listen up before it's too late! They're messin' with the ionosphere and jacking up our brainwaves! Wake up and smell the freedom fries, America! They're the ones causing all this chaos, so they can take over everything! We're talking mind control here. Just do your research! They want to turn us all into slaves!"

"Who's 'they'?" I inquired, as if the guy could hear me.

"We need to stand up to these bullies!" he thundered. "Tell your neighbors to quit acting like a bunch of mindless sheeple! Resist the tyranny now! Before it's too late!"

"Turn that nutcase off," Dad said.

I hit the "Off" button and smiled at my dad. "Takes one to know one."

"Very funny. C'mon, Gabs, let's go get some chow."

As we left the hotel room, I was kind of glad to have silenced RJ Hopper. Just the guy's frantic tone was upsetting in itself. He might be crazy, but there was no doubt the man believed every word he was saying.

Talk like that could freak you out, though, so I put him out of my mind. Maybe that made me one of the "mindless sheeple" he mentioned, but oh well. Besides, I'm only twelve. Even if what he said was true (which I doubted), what's a kid supposed to do about such things?

I shrugged it off, determined to enjoy my vacation.

Dad and I ate a quick breakfast, then drove our rental car over to the heliport. Our pilot's name was Ty. Cute, tan, outdoorsy. He'd have fit right in back home in California. We stowed our supplies and climbed aboard.

Ty and Dad were up front. I sat in the back. I closed my eyes as tightly as I could during liftoff. Pretended I was on an amusement park ride.

It really didn't feel any more jarring than an elevator going up—only much, much louder.

Eventually, I cracked open one eye and sneaked a peek out the window. I couldn't help but smile when I saw the snow-covered mountains. I hadn't seen snow since Dad took me skiing in Tahoe a couple of years ago.

It didn't take long for my fears to dissolve away to nothing. I'm glad I hadn't let on that I was scared. *Cool as a cucumber*, I thought, pleased with myself. Mom would be hyperventilating over my safety, but I felt brave.

It was hard to talk inside the cockpit due to all the noise. I didn't feel like wearing those silly headphones—I didn't want to mess up my hair—so I just gazed quietly at the endless beauty.

Wow. Seriously.

I could see for miles. It was a clear, sunny day. I was glad I had my shades on. The brilliant sunshine bouncing off the snowcaps and ocean would have been blinding otherwise. We headed southeast toward our destination, Glacier Bay National Park.

To my left, the land rose—towering, snowy mountains. To my right the water stretched as far as the eye could see—the Gulf of Alaska and the north Pacific, intensely blue.

At times, I spotted whales heaving up almost all the way out of the water. Maybe they were humpbacks, but I couldn't really tell. Dad had mentioned we were going to try to see some. Apparently the humpback whales travel every year from their breeding grounds in Hawaii to their favorite feeding places in

Alaska. That's some serious swimming, but what else do they have to do?

Dad was pointing and directing Ty so he could get the best video. He was in his element, filming almost nonstop. This wasn't the actual documentary, but the footage he'd show his financial backers to explain to them what he wanted to do and how much it was going to cost them.

I was taking quite a few pictures myself to show my friends back home. When Dad wasn't filming scenery, he would grab his camera, turn around, and take photos of me. I didn't mind because, after all, I couldn't wipe the smile off my face.

After about two hours, we headed down from the sky toward a little fishing village so Ty could refuel the helicopter. He told us no roads led there; the only way in or out was by air or sea. Talk about remote!

As we approached, I saw seaplanes as well as boats parked along the docks. In the center of the quaint, tiny town, the steeple of a Russian Orthodox church stuck up into the sky, with its trademark double-armed crosses. I had been surprised to learn that Alaska used to belong to Russia up until the mid-1800s, when America bought it from them.

I got out and stretched my legs while Ty filled up the chopper's gas tank, then it was back up into the air.

Three hours later, we reached our destination, did one quick flyover of the glacier—which was amazing—then landed.

It was good to be back on the ground.

We checked into the tourist-crammed lodge and crashed for several hours. Dad woke me up at nine p.m., and weirdly, it was still as light out as a typical afternoon.

The long hours of summer daylight in Alaska were a little hard to get used to. "Wake up, Spud, we're going for a hike to get some super footage of the sunset over the glacier."

"Sweet! Good idea, Dad."

I put on my hiking gear and went to meet him in the hallway. Dad gave me a plastic poncho in case it started raining. After all, like the posters in the lobby said, the southeastern region of Alaska was the largest temperate rainforest left in the world.

Before long, I was following my dad up into the green, mossy trails (and hoping we didn't see any bears).

It was a tough hike, uphill all the way, but the coolness of the air was refreshing, and when we found a good spot where we could see the glacier in the distance, the reward was well worth it.

The view went on forever.

The little campsite nearby had a ring of stones that meant bonfires were allowed in that spot. So, while Dad took video and photos of the not-quite-sunset, I gathered wood for a campfire. It was getting chilly up there.

The sun didn't set until, like, ten-thirty, and the sky still glowed for another hour after that.

Once it was finally somewhat dark, Dad put his cameras down and we sat and talked for a long time, sitting in front of the roaring campfire, just father and daughter, making s'mores and drinking hot chocolate.

He asked me questions about school. About boys. About how Mom was doing.

It was great to have him all to myself for a change. The

craziness felt a million miles away.

I was getting really tired, since it was now past midnight, when suddenly, I saw something utterly bizarre in the sky above the glacier.

"Whoa! What on earth is that?" I leaped to my feet and pointed at the freaky lights in the sky.

It was barely dark enough to see them. I immediately thought of that Tinfoil Hat guy on TV yelling about aliens.

But to my surprise, Dad laughed and quickly grabbed his camera. "That, my darlin' daughter, is the aurora borealis. Man, you must be my good luck charm! Huh. That's actually really weird."

"What do you mean?" I asked anxiously. Of course, I was thinking about the alien mother ship.

"You don't normally see them in July, especially this far south. But, hey, works for me." Then he went into narrator mode. "Behold, the northern lights."

With that, he repositioned his tripod and started clicking away.

Since there seemed to be no threat of little green men invading from Mars, I started to relax. "So, what is that, exactly? Why does it glow like that?"

"Well, I'm no geophysicist," Dad said as he kept on taking pictures, "but I do know that highly charged particles blow in on the solar wind. Once gravity pulls them into our atmosphere, the ions get attracted to the north and south poles. That's where the earth's magnetic fields are strongest. The ions just kind of hang out around the poles, mingling with the earth's electromagnetic energy. Colliding with atoms in the high atmosphere—and voilà.

Boogying lights."

"Dude." I shook my head.

"I know. Nature rocks," he said. "Now be quiet and let me work. I need to concentrate."

I nodded while he turned back into the obsessed filmmaker, lost in his own world.

So was I. I couldn't take my eyes off the aurora borealis. I just stood there staring in wonder.

Undulating waves of weird glowing colors filled the dark night sky, dancing like sheets on a clothesline—green, yellow, purple, pink. Over there, a streak of pale blue, a touch of red. Mother Nature was putting on a spectacular light show just for me and my dad.

"Wow," I breathed after a moment, dazzled. "Have you ever seen anything so beautiful in your life?"

Dad pulled himself away from his camera long enough to send me an endearing little smile. "Not since the day you were born, kid."

"Aw, Dad. You cheeseball!" I ran over and gave him a big hug.

He kissed me on the forehead, then told me to grab another lens out of his case. I went to get it with a shimmer of happy tears in my eyes. It really struck me in that moment how lucky I was to have two great parents, even if I didn't get to see one of them that often.

When he was satisfied with his footage, Dad finally put his camera away, then he came back to sit by the campfire with me. We just hung out on the mountaintop until the northern lights vanished as mysteriously as they had appeared.

It was one of the best times of my life.

Honestly, though, I would have begged to go back to San Francisco the very next day if I could have somehow known in advance what was going to happen to my poor dad.

Chapter 3
Orcas

"This is the life, eh, Spud?"

"Yeah, Dad. It sure is." I glanced over at him and smiled as the wind ran riot through our hair.

The next day, we were cruising at fifteen knots across Glacier Bay aboard a state-of-the-art research vessel called *The Blackfish*, whose main job was following killer whales up and down the Alaskan coast.

The beautiful forty-foot sailboat had sparkling white sails and a small crow's nest on the foremast as an observation post. I was dying to climb up to it.

Thankfully, the sailboat had a motor, too, in case we ran into bad weather or needed to get out of the way of any passing whales, which was the whole point of the day's mission.

Summer was humpback season in Glacier Bay, but Dad was more interested in getting some good dramatic footage of the resident orca pods.

"It'll help sell the bean counters on letting me make the

documentary. After all, everybody loves Shamu," he said in an easy tone, but the pretty lead scientist growled under her breath at the mention of the famous captive whale.

"Okaaay, maybe not everybody," Dad corrected himself.

"It's not Shamu I don't like, Mr. Reynolds," Dr. Jenny answered with a piercing look in her dark eyes. "It's the people who kidnap baby whales, take them from their pods, and keep them prisoner in man-made tanks for the rest of their lives."

With that, she tossed her long black hair over her shoulder and stalked off belowdecks, leaving us alone.

I glanced at my dad with a smirk.

He gave me a sheepish look. "Uh-oh. I think I offended our captain. Better go grovel a little so she doesn't heave me overboard."

"You like her, don't you, Dad?" I teased in a whisper. "I saw you staring at her."

"I just want her to agree to be one of the experts in my film!"

"Yeah, right. Too bad she doesn't like *you*."

"Please. Everybody likes me. Just watch." He put on his sunglasses, looking very Hollywood, and sauntered into the cabin after the research team's leader.

I shook my head in amusement.

While Dad worked on charming his way back into Dr. Jenny's good graces, I walked over to the side of the boat to have a look at the glorious day.

Alaska really was picture-perfect.

Bald eagles soared overhead. Porpoises leaped along through the waves. Sea lions sunned themselves on the rocks. Proud, white-capped mountains towered ahead of us in shades of purple, brown, and green. And between the peaks sat the glacier: a solid river of ice, glistening in pastel blue.

No wonder the whales come back every year, I thought as I walked along the deck toward the front of the boat. *This place is breathtaking.* I sat down on the bow, rested my chin on the metal rail, and dangled my feet over the side.

As I watched the waves gliding past, my mind wandered back to my mother's weird news during our phone conversation earlier that day. She had said that back home in the Lower 48, all of the riots had suddenly stopped just as abruptly as they had begun.

"It's like somebody pressed a button and shut them off, one city after another. It all just fizzled out. But it's kind of strange here still. Everyone out on the streets looks sort of stunned and confused. They're wandering around town like dazed..."

"Sheep?" The word had slipped out of my mouth before I realized I was quoting that "crazy" guy on the radio, RJ Hopper.

But really, why would weeks of riots across America just end like that unless somebody was purposely coordinating it?

My mother managed to tell me her theory despite her splitting headache. (Which was weird in itself. Mom's kind of a health nut and never gets headaches. She always brags about never getting sick.) "I think people are just finally coming to grips with the fact that this economy will take a long time to improve and we're all going to have to tighten our belts and make some sacrifices."

"Uh-huh," I had murmured skeptically.

"Who knows? Maybe they just needed to vent their frustrations and suddenly got tired of it all. What matters is that now things can finally get back to normal."

It sounded nice, but somehow I doubted it. Still, it was great to hear that people had stopped freaking out. That meant when I got home in a few days, I wouldn't have to be cooped up in my house again 24-7. There were only a few precious weeks of summer vacation left before I'd have to go back to school. *A prison of another type*, I thought, recalling my balcony view of Alcatraz.

The thought of school annoyed me. I got restless just thinking about sitting at a desk all day in that stuffy building, under those awful, ugly fluorescent lights.

After a few minutes, I decided to go below and make sure my dad wasn't driving Dr. Jenny crazy.

I walked across the gently rocking deck, ducked under the boom, then climbed down the steep, ladder-like steps into the boat's cabin.

There were padded benches all around and an assortment of little cubbyholes where gear and supplies could be stowed. There were electronic gadgets here and there and a bank of computers along the sidewall. I think it was portside, but I always get that mixed up with starboard.

The first person I saw was a bearded scientist in desperate need of a haircut and updated clothes. I would later find out that his name was Aaron. He was bopping back and forth between an oversized monitor and a loosely tacked map of the southern coast of Alaska. He barely noticed as I walked past and took a seat with my dad and Dr. Jenny at a rectangular table where the crew, I assumed, ate their meals. The two were drinking coffee and chatting. I quickly noticed that Dad had turned on the famous Chase Reynolds charm, full force.

And judging by Dr. Jenny's easygoing smile, I'd say it was working.

"So, what made you decide to study orca whales for a living?"

"Oh, it's in my blood," Dr. Jenny answered.

"How's that?"

"I'm a proud Tlingit woman, Mr. Reynolds. The killer whales are like our spiritual relatives."

"Rock on!" he said, offering her a fist bump.

She raised an eyebrow at his surfer-dude response but fist-bumped him back. Dr. Jenny looked bewildered, but amused.

I rolled my eyes. *He's such a flirt.*

"And please," he added sweetly, "call me Chase."

I sent him a private look, trying to warn him not to be annoying. He grinned back at me, looking about as mature as some of the boys in my class.

"So, how long does it usually take to find some whales?" I broke in, feeling a change of subject was definitely in order.

Dr. Jenny shrugged. "It just depends. There's a lot of waiting time involved in researching wildlife. You getting bored?"

"A little."

"Twelve-year-olds aren't big on waiting," Dad informed her.

"Well, maybe I can help entertain you until we find our orcas," Dr. Jenny said, giving me a big smile.

She slid off the bench and walked to the back of the cabin. A moment later, she returned and placed an electronic gadget on the table. It was about the size of my e-reader, only thicker.

"This is a hydrophone amp. Go ahead, pick it up. You won't break it."

"What does it do?" I asked as I inspected the device, then cautiously fiddled with its knobs and buttons.

"We hook a microphone with a long cable into that port. Then we throw the mic overboard, put on some headphones, and listen. We normally hear all kinds of sounds—boats, distant ships, military sonar, breaking waves. But we're trying to pick up the orcas' distinct whistles, clicks, and pops, so we can then home in on their location. Oh! And Mr. Reynolds—I mean, Chase—you'll love this."

She reached for a duffel bag and pulled out a high-end underwater camera. She handed it over.

"Sweet! Look at this little beauty," he said, spinning it every which way. "Oh, you are a fine piece of modern technology, aren't you? Now I know what I want for my birthday, Gabs."

"Dream on."

"When we find a pod, we use it to take pictures of the whales, for identification," Dr. Jenny explained while she grabbed a thick photo album from a nearby shelf. "We can usually tell them apart by the eye-patch and dorsal fin, which are all slightly different. Like a fingerprint. Here, have a look."

I started leafing through the pictures. "Good grief! This one's fin has got to be six feet high!" I glanced over at my dad. "Just the dorsal fin alone is as tall as you! I mean, I knew whales were big, but geez!"

"Actually, orcas aren't really whales at all," Dr. Jenny replied. "They're just wrongly called that. Believe it or not, killer whales are a supersized breed of dolphin."

"You're kidding!" I exclaimed.

"Nope. Animalia, Chordata, *mammalia, cetacea, odontoceti, delphinidea, orcinus, orca.*" She proudly rattled off the beast's scientific classification. "*Delphinidea* means *dolphin.*"

"Easy for you to say," my dad joked.

For better or for worse, over the next thirty minutes Dr. Jenny gave us the belowdecks grand tour. We shuffled through the cabin as she explained the high-tech vessel's communication systems, echo sounder, GPS device, electronic chart plotter, infrared night vision camera, Geiger radiation indicator, and EMF detection meter.

She was trying to speak in simple terms, and I really appreciated her attempt to be entertaining while we searched for the orcas, but after a while, I felt like I was in science class and became bored again.

The trained scientist with the keen eye for detail must have read my expression, because just as I was fighting back a yawn, Dr. Jenny clapped her hands together and said, "Hey, let's go topside! It's too gorgeous out to stay down here looking at all my equipment." She turned to me. "You want to go up on deck and do some real, hands-on scientific research, Gabby?"

"Sure!"

"C'mon. I'll give you a job to do. And Chase, grab the hydrophone. You can do some work for me, as well."

Dad did as he was told, and then we bounded up the ladder after our captain.

Up on deck, Dr. Jenny showed me how to take water samples, checking for such things as pH, ammonia, and nitrates.

She then worked with my dad on the underwater audio.

Having been engrossed in my task, I looked up several minutes later and was surprised to see a boatful of tourists waving at us from the large guide boat taking them around the bay.

Listening harder, I could just make out the muffled voice of their tour guide telling them about our vessel over the loudspeaker. "*The Blackfish* is a familiar sight along Alaska's coast, housing one of the premier research projects associated with the university. Interns from the Biology department can participate in field research. A once-in-a-lifetime experience..."

Whether they mistook me for a college kid intern from that distance or even one of the real researchers, I couldn't help feeling oh-so-important standing there taking the bay's pH reading.

I waved back.

"Hey, Gabby!" Dad yelled. "Come on over here for a minute. You've got to hear this."

I set the pH test tube and color card down and hurried to the back of the boat. "What's up?"

"Listen to how much noise the tourist boat makes," he said, handing me the headphones.

I pulled them over my ears and then winced in pain. It was thunderous. "That's horrible."

"I know." He shrugged.

Dr. Jenny spoke up. "Imagine what it's like for a whale to have to hear an even bigger boat, like a cruise ship, going past. Fortunately, the tour companies around here are usually respectful about not going too close to the whales, and they also cut the engines when they stop to look at them."

"So that's why you prefer the sailboat," I said.

She smiled and nodded. "Exactly. Nice and quiet." She let out a sigh. "You should see how whales and porpoises go into a panic when they're blasted with noise. It can still freak them out from over ten miles away. Their hearing is that sensitive, so such loud noise is deafening for them. That's a real problem, because they use echolocation for everything. Finding food. Talking to each other. Did you know their sonar is ten times more powerful than even humans' most advanced equipment? Oh, and don't even get me started on the Navy's ultrapowerful sonar testing. It pretty much blows out whales' and dolphins' eardrums."

Dr. Jenny told us how environmental groups had sued the Navy to try to restrict them from practicing their ultra-low-frequency sonar drills in whale breeding grounds.

"Oh yeah, some of those tests might be outside the range of human hearing, but we pick it up on our equipment, so it's not like they can deny it. I know the military has to practice and train—and I know the average Navy sailor loves the sea as much as I do. But if the top brass could see how cruel these kinds of tests are..." Her words trailed off. She seemed preoccupied by dark thoughts weighing on her mind.

"What is it?" Dad asked, studying her.

"Actually...we've been picking up some really weird EMF spikes lately that I honestly can't explain. Bizarre frequencies showing up on the livestream over the past few weeks. I almost wonder if the equipment's malfunctioning 'cause these readings can't be right. They're not possible."

He frowned. "What do you mean?"

"We'll get fluctuating radio and subradio bursts, which isn't all that unusual, but I'm also getting massive pulse frequencies in the microwave range at the exact same time. No ship is going to do that. And it's certainly not whales."

"Huh?" I asked, scrunching up my nose.

"That's about as weird as us seeing the aurora borealis last night," Dad remarked.

"What? You saw the aurora borealis? Here? In July?"

"Yep," Dad said.

"That's impossible," Dr. Jenny said.

"I'm a trained observer, Jenny. I know what I saw. Plus, I've got the footage, if you don't believe me."

"I believe you. It's just... Hmm."

The two adults gazed at each other, both looking confused and a little troubled. Then the marine biologist gave another perplexed shrug. "I don't know what could have produced those wacky readings. I've been on the phone with my Navy contacts screaming at them to tell me what kind of tests they're doing that could generate that output, but they swear that nothing's going on. They claim to know nothing about it." She paused, visibly struggling to make sense of it. "It's probably just the boat's equipment malfunctioning, right?"

"Hard to say," Dad answered as delicately as if he was approaching a leopard in the brush. "Have you checked with any other whale researchers in your network?"

"No, but I could try."

Just then, Aaron poked his head out through the cabin door with a grin from ear to ear. "Guess who just showed up on the sonar? We've got orcas!"

"Yay!" I instinctively grabbed hold of my dad's hand, half in excitement and half in fear.

He laughed at me, but I didn't let go.

They weren't called killer whales for nothin'.

Chapter 4
The Distress Call

"Dad, *please* be careful! You're gonna fall in!" I hollered. He was leaning out over the railing, his video camera trained on the orca pod ahead.

"You're starting to sound like your worrywart mom. Man, are they gorgeous or what? Absolutely *magnificent*!" Dad let out a howl like a crazed football fan whose team was about to win the championship.

Told you he was nuts.

I hung back from the railing, heart pounding. I had no desire to stand so close to the edge, with the greatest predator in the seven seas swimming fifty yards off the bow.

The Blackfish drifted slowly toward the orcas.

"What am I gonna tell your fan club if you get eaten, Dad?"

He laughed. "They're not great white sharks, Gabby."

"Actually, they eat great whites," Dr. Jenny remarked. But Dad wasn't listening because as she was talking, one of the orcas popped straight up out of the water, hung in midair for a split second, then crashed down on its side.

"Woo-hoo!" he shouted.

"That's called breaching. It's playful and looks fun, but it's also how they remove parasites from their skin," Dr. Jenny said, ever the scientist. "Oh, look, there's Bubbles," she said as a second orca breached even closer but not as high.

"Bubbles?" I said.

"Yeah, Bubbles is the matriarch—the head female. The ladies rule the roost in the orca world, Gabby. Did you know that?"

"No, but cool. Girl power!"

As several more orcas joined in the frolicking, Dr. Jenny explained the intricacies of the pod. "This is the world famous A-Pod. Bubbles is the oldest at fifty-two, so therefore, she's the boss. Whatever she says goes. There are nineteen members of the group total. Brothers, sisters, sons, daughters, nephews, nieces, cousins, and grandbabies. Three generations, all related, all living together."

"And they all get along?" I asked, thinking of how my own parents bickered whenever they saw each other.

"Yeah, for the most part. Their social structure is really complex but interesting. For example, the older females stay with their grown whale daughters and help look after the babies. We call them granny whales. There are three granny whales in the A-Pod: Bubbles and her sisters, Pancake and Star. We believe they help teach the young how to go about doing things in the group. All pods are different, you see. They have their own language, their own hunting grounds. Different pods even choose to eat different foods."

"Really?"

She nodded. "Some will only eat fish and sea birds. Some prefer seals."

"And some prefer human flesh, *muahaha*," Dad taunted me, taking his eyes off the beasts only for a second. Long enough for me to send him a scowl.

"As I was saying," Dr. Jenny continued, turning slightly away from my dad. Smart lady—she was already learning to ignore him. "All pods are different. They even have their own hobbies. Seriously! We know of one group that likes swimming along the bottom of a pebble beach in the shallows, rubbing their bellies on the rocks. We have no idea why."

"Weird! Marking their territory like a cat?"

She shrugged, smiling. "Not likely. Maybe it just feels good on their skin."

"How funny!"

"I know. They all have their own little personalities."

"Little?" I echoed wryly.

"Yeah, maybe not the best word when it comes to orcas. Anyway, you see now why I get so angry about theme parks taking baby whales away from their mothers. Even if you can eventually get the park to release the animal back into the wild, once they get out there, they're totally alone. They have no pod to hunt with. They don't even know *how* to hunt, since they've been fed by people all their lives! This leaves them helpless. They can't talk to any other whales to learn what to do, either, because there's no shared language. And since they're outsiders, other whales will often treat them like an enemy, even attack them. They're out there alone with no idea what to do."

"How sad."

"I know. Whales need to be in families, just like people." Maybe Dr. Jenny realized she was totally depressing me, for she looked at me, then smiled brightly. "Let's see if we can hear what they're saying today." She lowered the hydrophone into the water and then removed the headphones so we could listen in speaker mode. "You'll want to listen for clicks and calls, that sort of thing."

I walked over and leaned my ear toward the device.

We soon heard them. It was amazing. You really would expect something as scary as a killer whale to make intimidating sounds—I don't know, growls or something—but amid the bubbly, gurgly sounds of the waves, squeaky trills and rapid-fire chirps began coming out of the speaker.

"What are they saying?" I asked Dr. Jenny as she adjusted the buttons to fine-tune the sound.

"Probably just discussing where the food is hiding." She paused, listening. "Hmm. Actually, they sound kind of upset."

"How can you tell? Do they have a specific distress call?"

"It's more the way they say it—the high pitches and quick speeds of their calls. They sound a little agitated. Yeah, something is definitely bothering them."

"Maybe an enemy is in the area?" I suggested as she walked over to the railing.

"Orcas have no natural enemies...well, except people." She lifted her binoculars up to her eyes. "There's Simon and Wavy and Giggles." She pointed them out. The whales swam slowly in a cluster near the surface. Their huge dorsal fins were terrifying. "Hmm, Lightning ought to be around here somewhere. You have got to see Lightning. He's huge—largest in the pod. Huh, that's weird. He always hangs out with his brother, Giggles."

"How can you seriously call a twenty-foot death machine 'Giggles'?" I asked in amusement.

"Because that's what his vocalizations sound like. See? There he is now!" Dr. Jenny gestured toward the speaker as we heard a few short notes of a playful-sounding staccato call.

I grinned. "Yeah, they kinda do."

"Not sounding as happy as usual, though. I wonder what's bugging him."

One of the whales came within ten yards of the boat, angled his body upward and rolled to the side a little, lifting one eye above the surface. I watched its eyeball dart from side to side as it took a good look around. I stared back, flabbergasted. "He's looking right at us!" I waved in spite of myself. "Hi, whaley!"

Dr. Jenny laughed. "Hello, Blaze! Yes, we see you, too. Such a handsome boy!"

"That's a good-looking whale," Dad remarked, filming nonstop. "Smile, buddy."

"Blaze is the curious one of the bunch," Dr. Jenny said affectionately, as if she was talking about her own family members. "He's only five—the youngest in the pod. Little rascal, that one."

"Little? He's ginormous!"

"He's nowhere near full-grown. He'll grow to be nearly thirty feet long when he's an adult and weigh six tons like his uncle Lightning. Where is Lightning, anyway? If we can find him, then you can compare that little squirt to a full-grown male." While she continued talking, she scanned the bay with her binoculars. "As you can see, they're not shy. They've gotten pretty used to encountering humans out here—"

Her words stopped abruptly as the hydrophone picked up a chilling sound that one of the whales suddenly made.

I turned to Dr. Jenny. "What was that?"

The color had drained from her face. Rather than answering, she turned the speaker up louder and listened until the whale made the noise again.

A long, sorrowful, haunting moan.

Dad looked over at Dr. Jenny, all the humor vanished from his face. "Are you sure about these whales not having a distinct distress call?"

"I've never heard them make that sound before."

Even I could tell that it sounded as if something was wrong. "Maybe they're asking for our help," I ventured.

Scanning the horizon through her binoculars, Dr. Jenny suddenly went motionless. "Oh no."

"What is it?" Dad asked.

"Oh...no, no, please." The whole atmosphere aboard *The Blackfish* changed in an instant. "Steven, get me over to that pebble beach as fast as you can." She pointed. *"Now!* Aaron, get NOAA on the comm! Give them our coordinates and tell them we need them out here with at least two or three refloat teams and a backhoe ASAP!"

"Jenny, what is it?" Dad asked quickly.

Then she said the words that had to be every whale researcher's nightmare. "We've got a mass stranding on our hands. I found Lightning. He's stuck on that beach with three other whales."

I drew in my breath.

Within seconds, the first mate fired up the sailboat's small motor with a roar. I held on, frightened and confused, steadying myself against the rocking of the boat.

I thought of that haunting sound we'd heard again. Maybe the whales really had been asking Dr. Jenny for her help.

Dad stopped filming, backed away from the railing, and put his arm around me. We both stayed out of the way while the research team raced about the boat getting everything ready for a desperate whale rescue.

Before long, we were gliding up to a remote, rocky spit of land where four of the A-Pod whales had somehow managed to beach themselves as the tide went out.

I stared in dismay.

The massive black-and-white creatures looked dead to me. I didn't see any movement. Grimly, Dad resumed filming.

When we reached the lonely stretch of wild beach, Dr. Jenny leaped off the boat and ran through the shallows, holding a first-aid kit. Most of her crew members followed while Steven threw down the anchor.

Dad and I went ashore as well, ready to help in any way we could. I was shocked at how massive the orcas were out of the water.

Racing up alongside the four motionless beached whales, Dr. Jenny and her crew started frantically checking the orcas' vital signs. I stayed out of the way, but from where I stood, it didn't look good.

"Hey! Lightning's still alive!" one of the crew members yelled from beside the most gigantic one. There was a twinge of hope in his voice. Everyone descended on the only living orca and raced to try to save its life.

Dad put down his camera, and we both joined the rescue effort, following the experts' instructions.

"Aaron, get on the radio again and find out how long it's gonna take them to get here!" Dr. Jenny yelled to her assistant. "Everybody, roll up your sleeves. We need to dig the sand and gravel out from around him so he can breathe better."

We scrambled to do as she said. It was then that I noticed how much the whale was struggling to inhale and the pained expression in its eyes. I felt a coldness in my heart, fearing deep down that we were fighting a losing battle.

A few minutes later, Aaron came back, his face pale as he reported that the rescue team from NOAA estimated it would take them six hours to ferry a backhoe out to this remote corner of Glacier Bay.

"Six hours? He'll never last that long!" Dr. Jenny burst out.

"Come on, we've got to keep trying," Dad urged.

We redoubled our efforts.

I frantically dug sand, dirt, and rocks out from around Lightning's sleek black flanks with my bare hands.

Dad switched jobs and was assisting in the battle to keep the orca's skin wet. The researchers had placed soaking wet towels all over the whale's back and flippers. My dad was running back and forth, dumping buckets of water all over Lightning's enormous frame.

As the crew worked, Dr. Jenny continued to monitor the orca's heart rate with a stethoscope. She was petting his head and staring into his big, weary brown eyes. I could hear her talking sweetly to him. It seemed to calm the whale down considerably.

But ultimately, we had found the stranded beast too late.

The struggling orca breathed his last.

I started to cry when Dr. Jenny told us all to stop.

"He's gone. Tell NOAA never mind." The head marine biologist threw down her equipment, wiped away a tear, and walked off to be by herself.

It seemed so needless, horrible and cruel, and such a waste of these magnificent creatures' lives.

I couldn't understand how they had gotten themselves into such a position. You'd think whales would be pretty good at swimming and have the sense not to get stuck on a beach.

Dad came over, dripping wet, and gave me a hug. All the researchers were distraught, considering how they had come to know each member of the A-Pod nearly as well as the people they worked with every day.

"Poor orcas," Aaron said sadly. "They deserve better than this. Thank God none of the new mothers were among them. The babies can't survive without their moms. But still, a loss like this is just...devastating."

A few yards away, Dr. Jenny tilted her face to the sky and murmured something in the old tongue of her people, honoring the newly deceased orcas' spirits.

\# \# \#

"Why did they do that to themselves?" I asked a little while later, my eyes still red from crying.

The Blackfish was back out to sea, but the mood on the research vessel had definitely changed.

Dr. Jenny shook her head. "It's hard to say, Gabby. If it were just one whale, I'd say it was an accident, that the poor thing might've been hit by a boat or just swam into water that was too shallow without noticing. But not when there are four of them. This is the kind of thing that happens after those Navy tests that I described earlier."

"The Navy did this?" I exclaimed.

"No, they wouldn't be testing right here in the bay," she said uncertainly.

"Then who else could it be?"

"Maybe it's got something to do with those strange readings you mentioned," Dad spoke up.

Dr. Jenny sent him a dark glance. "I'm afraid you may be right. I can't think of anything else that it could be. The microwaves, the radio waves, the ELFs, the pulsing combination of all three frequencies, who knows? I'm at a loss."

"I've heard of microwaves and radio waves, but what are ELF waves?" I asked.

"Extremely Low Frequency waves, also called subradio waves," Dr. Jenny answered. "Since ELF waves can travel really far underwater, the military uses them to communicate with submarines all over the world. It's controversial because they've been known to throw off whales' echolocation systems. The whales get all confused."

"That explains how those four whales could have swum straight up onto a beach," I mumbled with a frown. "But where do these ELF waves come from?"

"That's the most disturbing part. Long subradio frequencies should mostly be found in the deep oceans, sent from Navy vessel to Navy vessel. It's not safe to generate them near human population centers."

"Why?" I asked.

"Overexposure to ELFs is harmful to humans. It can give people headaches, hallucinations, brain fog, and other weird side effects. But here's the thing..." Dr. Jenny glanced from me to Dad. "One of the few facilities on land where they *can* create all three types of signals—microwaves, radio waves, and ELF waves—is right here in Alaska, just south of Fairbanks. It's called the Northern Lights lab."

"Well, isn't that convenient," Dad drawled. "That's just a few hundred kilometers away."

"That can't be a coincidence," I said.

Dr. Jenny gave a wary shrug. "From what I'm told, aside from serving as a signal station to the submarines, the researchers up there are just studying the aurora borealis. The ionosphere. Solar wind. Sky stuff."

Anger blazed in Dad's eyes. "Maybe we ought to go have a talk with them about the environmental impact of whatever it is they're messing around with up there."

Dr. Jenny bit her lip. "I don't know, Chase. It's not like you can just walk in there and start asking questions. Northern Lights has got some pretty formidable security."

"What for?" I asked dubiously. "I mean, if they're just studying pretty lights in the sky...?"

They both looked at me.

I might be only twelve, but my mom isn't raising a fool.

"Good question, Gabs." Dad put on his Hollywood shades once more. But there was a grim set to his mouth. "Let's pick this up later, all right? It's been a tough day. The kid's had enough, I think. We should be getting back."

Dr. Jenny nodded.

I was glad to go.

Chapter 5

Bad Dreams

Dad wasn't in the mood to film anymore as we made our way back to the dock. I couldn't really blame him. That *was* upsetting. I had heard that whales and dolphins would sometimes beach themselves, but I couldn't believe we had just witnessed it firsthand.

As much as I would have liked to rid it from my brain, it was the sort of memory that would stay with me for the rest of my life.

Anyway, within an hour we were back at the lodge. Dad and Dr. Jenny decided to get some coffee, but I told them I wanted to go up to my room for a while.

Still disturbed about the whales, I needed better answers about what had happened today. I quickly fired up the computer. At least the Wi-Fi was working. I did a search on ELF waves, and sheesh, did I ever get more than I bargained for.

Propped up by a bunch of pillows against the headboard, I skimmed through dozens of online articles. To my great surprise, I found several that said ELFs could be used for sinister purposes. In particular, mind control.

"You have got to be kidding me," I said under my breath.

Before long, I found myself reading commentaries posted on the website of none other than the local radio "nutcase" himself, RJ Hopper.

I almost didn't want to admit it, but the more I read, the more his rant on the radio was starting to make sense.

He was obsessed with the New World Order, whatever that was, and positively freaked out by the Northern Lights lab. The bloggers on his website all seemed to agree on a few basic points about the facility:

"High security, little public access."

"Nobody really knows what goes on there."

"Covert experimental technologies."

"Weather weapons. Mind control."

"Alaska's version of Area 51."

Holy heck, I thought, wide-eyed as I read.

Maybe I had absorbed a little too much crazy from reading the blog posts, but dark notions were churning in my mind.

There was a "Contact" button on his website, so before I lost my nerve, I decided to write the radio host a quick e-mail.

Dear Mr. Hopper,

Hi, my name is Gabby. I'm on a video shoot in Alaska with my dad, Chase Reynolds, the wildlife documentary filmmaker. I want to ask you a question.

We were out on a boat today filming the whales when we saw something horrible. There were dead orcas on the beach. Well, one was alive still, but it died, too. We couldn't save it.

The marine biologists we were with said that they've been getting unexplainable ELF readings on their meter thingy all season. We started wondering if the ELF waves could have been the cause of the orcas beaching themselves.

I haven't said anything to my dad yet, but if these waves can travel all the way to deepwater submarines on the other side of the earth, and if they're powerful enough to scramble the whales' brains like that, then is it possible that somebody could be aiming ELF waves at targeted cities and causing all these crazy riots going on in the lower 48? You know, like an enemy nation or something.

I mean, maybe we're under attack and we don't even know it. I guess that sounds kind of insane. Well, just thought I'd ask. Thank you for your time.

Gabby Reynolds

Right after I hit "Send," the whole thing started to sound really nutty to me. So I went to Northern Lights' official website, expecting to feel like even more of an idiot, because surely you could trust these nice government scientists.

On the homepage, the smiling, lab-coated researchers in the photo did not seem the slightest bit evil.

Their website innocently stated that the primary purpose of their research facility was to study the aurora borealis phenomenon, hence the lab's name, Northern Lights. They also pioneered cutting-edge global communication systems.

I frowned, staring at the screen.

With all the conspiracy theories running around in my head, their bland reassurances sounded fishy to me. Was this the truth or just some kind of a cover story?

Feeling even more paranoid, I searched for images of the Northern Lights facility and found only grainy satellite pictures that didn't really show anything.

Weird.

Ready to wrap it up for the night, I checked my e-mail one last time and was shocked to see I had already gotten a response from Mr. Hopper.

He wrote only a few words in answer to my question: *Pulsed with microwaves, ABSOLUTELY! Keep digging. Start here...*

He sent me a link to a scientific research article by a Dr. Kelvin Mackowsky. I clicked on the link right away.

I tried to read it, I really did, especially since the introduction to the article claimed it had been leaked by a secret source in the Pentagon. But the equations and scientific jargon were so hard to grasp and so boring it nearly made my brain leak out of my ears like it wanted to escape.

In plain English, the gist of it—or the best that I could gather—was that Dr. Mackowsky believed the Northern Lights' giant grid of radio antennas could be tweaked to send out *other* kinds of signals. He gave a number of scary examples.

Instead of sending ELFs into the sea to reach submarines, he said the waves could be aimed at the sky to drive big wallops of energy to bow out the ionosphere in places. Which, in turn, would mess with the weather. He claimed you could steer a hurricane wherever you wanted it to go with that kind of technology.

That way, the weather itself could be turned into a weapon. He explained how you could dry up the rain clouds to cause a drought anywhere on earth that you chose. On the flip side, you could supercharge the atmosphere or something, causing storms to bring flooding, which could wreck an enemy nation's crops, and by such means, he very thoughtfully pointed out, you could starve a population into submission. Only in a war scenario, of course.

"Sheesh, nice guy," I said under my breath.

Dr. Mackowsky went on to explain how the harnessed energy beams could be bounced off the ionosphere to ricochet down to the earth at any location you wanted, like a giant fist slamming into the earth's crust. Doing *that* could theoretically cause an earthquake.

I gulped as I thought of San Francisco and my mom and all my friends back home. Everybody knows that one day, the *big one* is probably going to hit.

But Dr. Mackowsky had saved the best for last.

He explained how the human brain, in fact the whole body, continuously gives off a field of electrical energy. But there's this weird phenomenon called Brainwave Entrainment.

Our brains apparently like to get in sync with whatever dominant frequencies are around us—literally putting us on the same wavelength with whatever waves are around us at any given time.

Dr. Mackowsky theorized that through this little quirk of the human brain, you could use different frequencies to basically hack into people's minds and mess with them. It wasn't mind control, per se, but a kind of invisible mood attack on some unsuspecting person.

He claimed that by using a device such as a giant antenna array like the one at Northern Lights, you could carry out such an attack on distant lands. Simply take aim at a faraway city, fire an electromagnetic energy beam—preferably in the microwave range of the spectrum—at the sky, bounce the signal off the ionosphere at just the right angle, and boom!

You could fill the streets of that city with the wavelengths that would start making people's brains get in sync with your signal. Nobody would ever be the wiser, for the frequencies being launched at the people were out of the range of human perception. You couldn't see them, couldn't hear them, and yet, all the same, they could have all kinds of weird effects on the people in that area.

Like causing them to riot and flip out at the cops? I wondered.

"This is so messed up," I whispered to myself. *Way scarier than the stupid aliens the Tinfoil Hat people are worried about.*

I wished it *were* just aliens.

A chill ran down my spine as a terrifying thought gripped my mind. What if all the riots had been just one gargantuan scientific experiment? But it was coming from a government facility... Geez, they were supposed to be the good guys! But what if we were just their little lab rats and these egghead government scientists were studying us, just to see how we'd react?

Gulp.

Maybe I should e-mail this Dr. Mackowsky guy next, I thought. But by that point, I was too freaked out to type.

He'd probably just laugh at me and say I was just a goofy kid with an overactive imagination, and that it was all theoretical, anyway.

Maybe the guy didn't even know what he was talking about. *Yeah,* I thought, trying to talk myself down off the ledge, *he's probably just some bald, aging professor type.*

I was still sitting there, ashen-faced, when Dad casually sauntered into the room. "Hey, Spud. How you doing, honey? That was pretty sad today, huh?"

"Yeah." I nodded. "I'm okay, I guess."

He smiled. "That's my girl. Hey, I was just talking with Ty. We're going to pack up and head back to Anchorage first thing in the morning. So get most of your stuff packed before you get some shuteye." He furrowed his brow and looked closer at me. "You sure you're all right?"

"Yeah, just tired."

After his dismissive reaction to hearing RJ on the radio, I was not ready to share what I had just learned.

"You should get some sleep. Love ya, sweetie." He gave me a squeeze on the shoulder and strolled to the doorway. Then he turned back. "Oh, by the way, Dr. Jenny's going to fly out with us tomorrow."

"Sheesh, Dad, that was fast," I blurted out.

"What?" He practically blushed.

Busted!

"We're just giving her a ride back to Anchorage, that's all. It's not what you think." He gave me a sheepish look.

"None of *my* business."

"She's going to see if she can set up a chance for me to meet some of her tribe's elders. How cool is that?"

"You like her. Oh, it's okay. I approve. She's nice."

"Good night, Gabby," he said with a pointed smile.

"Good night, Dad," I called pleasantly as he left.

I guess the wild Chase Reynolds doesn't meet many women who are as fearless in the great outdoors as he is. But Dr. Jenny had some serious guts, considering that she frequently went diving with the killer whales.

Both of them are crazy.

Anyway, the brief visit with my dad made me feel a bit better about all the weirdness I had unearthed. So I closed my laptop, got up, and stretched for a minute, then I quickly packed up all my stuff. I was kind of glad to be leaving Glacier Bay after the depressing episode with the orcas.

# # #

We got underway early the next morning. As we lifted off this

58

time, I wasn't scared of the helicopter one bit. I even decided to wear the headphones.

It's hard to worry about messing up your hair, after all, when some laboratory filled with psycho nerds could be out there shooting invisible beams at people.

After sleeping on the matter, I decided I had to tell the others about what I had learned in my research.

While cruising back to Anchorage, following the shoreline at a hundred miles per hour, I explained to everyone onboard as much as I knew about Northern Lights and Dr. Mackowsky's theories.

"So, you see," I concluded, "this could turn out to be even bigger than what happened to those poor whales."

I waited, wide-eyed, for their reactions.

My dad turned around in the cockpit and stared at me for a second. He didn't say anything, and I couldn't read him. I only saw my own worried face, distorted, in the reflection of his mirrored sunglasses.

He let out a sigh and turned forward again. He shook his head, lifted his sunglasses a bit, and rubbed his eyes like he was striving for patience. "Where did you say you found this so-called scientific paper?"

"Somebody sent me a link," I said a tad defensively.

"Who?" he demanded.

"Oh, fine!" I said, and told him. "It was RJ Hopper."

He reacted about as well as I expected, half mocking, half furious. "No wonder you sound so ridiculous!"

"Thanks, Dad."

"Gabby, stuff like that doesn't happen. There's no weather

weapon, no mind-control machine, and I certainly don't want my twelve-year-old daughter contacting the King Kook Conspiracy Nut himself! Northern Lights might have caused a couple of orcas to get stuck on the beach, but come on...you're taking this too far. That guy's filling your head with all kinds of nonsense. The government attacking its own people? Reality check time!"

I was startled and stung. He never yells at me.

Dr. Jenny spoke up cautiously after a second. "Actually, Chase..." She shrugged. "Rumors have been circulating about that place for years."

"Not you, too!" He scowled at her, then rapped Ty on the arm. "You don't believe all this junk, do you? You were born in Alaska, right?"

"Lived here all my life except when I was in the Army."

"Then back me up here, man."

Ty shrugged. "It is restricted airspace. That's all I know. Other than that, I'm staying out of it." He smiled at me over his shoulder.

"Well, that's just awesome." Laughing at us, my dad started singing the theme song from the old *X-Files* show. "Somebody call Mulder and Scully. Doo-doo-doo-doo-doo-doooo..."

I folded my arms across my chest, scowled at the back of his head, and gave up for now, but I couldn't help wondering if my own dad was one of the "sheeple" Mr. Hopper liked to rant about.

It was still light out when we finally landed in Anchorage. *Big surprise, it's almost always light out*, I thought. Was it night? Day? The continuous daylight was starting to get to me. It was very disorienting.

We said goodbye to Ty and Dr. Jenny and headed straight to the hotel. I was still annoyed with my dad for yelling and then laughing at me, so I didn't protest when he decided to get a sandwich at the lobby pub before going to his room across the hall from mine.

All the motion of the helicopter ride had left me a little dizzy and I wasn't hungry, so I went directly to the elevator.

I was not in the best mood, what with my dad making fun of me, and the whole Northern Lights conspiracy rattling around in my head.

I made my way up to my room and slammed the door shut, perhaps a little too hard. I quickly changed into my pajamas, pulled the shades tightly closed to block out the endless sun, and hopped into bed for a long, restless sleep.

But when I finally drifted off, I dreamed that the *big one* hit San Francisco, and the edge of the continent cracked off, and Mom and me and everyone I had ever known fell into the sea.

Chapter 6
The Coconspirators' Café

The next morning (at least I thought it was morning), sitting at a small table in my hotel room in a much better mood, I fired up my computer and found a second e-mail from RJ Hopper. As soon as I read it, I knew my dad wasn't going to like what it said.

The larger-than-life radio personality was requesting to send a couple of his team members to Anchorage that very night to meet with me and my dad. He said he wanted his associates to ask us some questions and that dinner would be his treat—anything we wanted to eat.

As I sat there staring blankly at the screen, feeling confused about everything that had happened and everything that I had learned, and wondering what Mr. Hopper could possibly want to ask the two of us, there was a knock at the door.

"Morning, sunshine. It's a beautiful day. Wakey, wakey. You up?" my dad asked.

I walked over to the door and let him in.

"I'm up."

"Brought you some breakfast." He sauntered over and set a brown bag on the table next to my laptop. "Whatcha up to?"

"Oh, just running around the Internet."

"Cool. Are your friends back online?" he asked as he started pulling food out. It smelled heavenly. "Or are they still bored little prisoners?"

"Come on, old man," I teased, "you know nobody under the age of twenty *e-mails* their friends. They would text me, which, no, I haven't heard from them. Cell service stinks here, so I turned my phone off. It's frustrating."

"Well, come, have some grub. You must be starving. You skipped dinner last night. You're too skinny to go missing meals."

"I am hungry, thanks." I sat down and unwrapped an egg-and-cheese bagel. Took a few bites. "I did get this one e-mail, though."

"Oh?" He eyed me skeptically, taking a sip of coffee.

Chase Reynolds is pretty slick. I figured he had a good idea where I was going, so between mouthfuls, I just blurted it out. "RJ Hopper's team wants to buy us dinner tonight and ask us a few questions. Free meal! Whaddya say? You in?"

He thought about it for perhaps a millisecond and snapped back, "No way, Gabby. Why are you still communicating with that guy?"

"I'm not. He e-mailed *me*! I haven't responded yet. I wanted to talk to you first to see what you'd say." I folded my arms across my chest. "I guess I got my answer. But actually, I'm kind of surprised at you, Dad."

"Don't give me that look, Gabby. You have no idea what

63

you're getting yourself into. People with extreme beliefs go to crazy measures to make their points. These wack jobs might be dangerous!"

"Don't you think you might be overreacting a little? They're not dangerous, Dad. They're radio talkers, not terrorists! Besides, you love danger."

"No, I don't. I take calculated risks."

"Who are you kidding?"

"And what could they possibly want to talk to us about?"

"Not sure. Probably what we can do to help save the whales. That's all. Come on, Dad. This would mean so much to me! Yesterday was horrible, the way those whales died. And besides, if we uncover information to help save the A-Pod, you could score some brownie points with Dr. Jenny."

He sent a stern look my way. "Don't even go there."

"Seriously! You always get to go on these grand adventures and do exciting, wild things. Can't I have a little adventure, too?"

"You're in Alaska, aren't you? You flew in a helicopter."

"I know, but this is different. Please, Dad. Can't we just meet them? If things start getting weird or scary or dangerous, just say the word and we're out of there. I promise. It's gonna be in a public restaurant, anyway. It's safe."

He mulled it over for a moment while scarfing the rest of his bagel.

"Oh, all right!" He grabbed a chocolate donut. "But if I see one sliver of tinfoil, we're gone!"

"That's a deal!" I shouted and leaped to my feet. I couldn't resist getting up and giving him a big hug. "Thanks, Dad."

After breakfast, I sent a quick e-mail response to Mr.

Hopper. It wasn't long before he sent us our instructions. We were to meet his producer, a man named Kyle, and one of his techies at a place called the Bearded Seal Restaurant on Third Avenue at seven sharp.

Kyle would be sitting out on the patio wearing a farmer's straw hat so we could easily pick him out of the crowd. We were told to walk over to the table as casually as possible and not to draw any unnecessary attention to ourselves. He claimed he and his team were frequently under government surveillance.

We spent a good portion of the morning cleaning Dad's equipment and the entire afternoon just doing touristy things in downtown Anchorage, "The City of Lights and Flowers."

I couldn't wait for our meeting. The excitement was building all day.

At seven on the nose, we walked into the Bearded Seal. The restaurant had a casual vibe. Classic rock filled the dining room while waiters and waitresses scurried around wearing black jeans and white button-downs.

We told the hostess that we were meeting our friends on the patio and stepped outside. The space was three-quarters full and had a great view of the water.

"There's the straw hat, Dad," I whispered. I put my hands in my pockets and shifted my gaze to the ground.

He rolled his eyes at my effort to look inconspicuous. "Come on, Gabby. You're being silly."

We made our way over to the table. It was in the corner, out of the main flow of the customers. There were two other people sitting with the man in the straw hat.

"Kyle?" Dad asked.

The man looked up, his expression stern. He stared at us for a moment with a piercing gaze. He was reading us, sizing us up—friend or foe.

I guess he decided friend because after an uncomfortable moment or two, he stood up, whipped off his hat, and shoved his hand toward my dad. "Chase Reynolds, I'm RJ Hopper. Nice to meet you."

"It's you!" I exclaimed, recognizing the raspy voice.

Dad looked surprised but quickly recovered and shook the man's hand. The same man he had called the King Kook Conspiracy Nut only yesterday.

I have to admit, he did look a little nutty standing there in brown combat boots, green shorts, and a green button-down, as if he were heading out on a safari right after dessert.

Next, Mr. Hopper reached out to shake *my* hand. "You must be Gabby?" His grip was firm, and he held on overly long with a big, goofy smile on his face.

Mr. Hopper quickly introduced the other two people at the table: Kyle Yackberg, the producer, and Raven Gilkinson, the chief engineer.

Kyle was friendly and seemed nice enough. He was a hippie sort of dude, wearing a green alien T-shirt with the words *I Believe* printed along the bottom. Raven, on the other hand, was all edgy and goth, with black nail polish, pink streaks in her midnight hair, and dangling skeleton earrings. She seemed quiet and reserved.

Very inconspicuous outfits, guys.

We sat down and ordered drinks.

"I thought this was too important to leave to my team," Mr.

Hopper explained, "so I decided to make the drive and see you myself."

Not wasting any time, Dad leaned in toward the man and got right to the point. "What would you like to ask us, Mr. Hopper?"

"Oh, please, call me RJ. Let's talk for a while, get to know each other," he said with a devilish spark in his eye, "and then I will tell you what's on my mind."

Dad leaned back, looking slightly disappointed.

RJ Hopper could talk. Even with a mouthful of food, the man hardly took a breath. I guess that was why he went into radio.

Fortunately for everyone at the table, he had so much enthusiasm and intensity about everything he spoke about—it didn't matter the topic—he was entertaining.

After a while, I noticed that I actually had something in common with RJ Hopper: we both were fidgety and had a hard time sitting still. Amazingly, his level of squirminess far exceeded mine. Whereas I could stop fidgeting and keep it under control if I had to, RJ was bouncing around and touching everything all through dinner, nonstop.

He slid in his chair so much I thought all four of its legs were going to fall off. He kind of reminded me of the hyperactive boys at school who were always tapping their pencils, banging on the walls, mumbling to anyone who was near even if they weren't interested in talking, constantly asking to go to the bathroom, and pretty much driving the teachers bonkers. I bet when Mr. Hopper was little, he drove his teachers bonkers, too.

We talked about all kinds of things in a directionless parade of topics. Dad's work, my boring summer, the riots, the economy, the beached whales, Alaska, travel, sports, movies, you name it.

By the time we finished dessert, I decided RJ was totally cool. He was so personable that it was hard *not* to like the man. I could tell Dad liked him, too, in spite of himself. They were talking as if they were old friends who hadn't seen each other in years.

And not once did I see a sliver of tinfoil.

Over coffee, the radio guy with the loud, booming voice spoke using an indoor voice for the first time that night. I was surprised he *had* an indoor voice. "Okay, you two, let's talk business."

The moment had arrived. I could hardly contain my excitement, but I played it cool.

"I have to admit, when I got the e-mail from Gabby, I had Raven run a background check on the both of you. Pretty standard stuff for paranoids like me who get multiple death threats every day. Please don't be offended."

I certainly wasn't. Dad didn't look too concerned either. That was, until Raven spoke up.

"Careful with all that stuff you're claiming as tax write-offs, Chase," she mumbled while tucking a loose strand of pink hair behind her ear. "Some of it would be considered personal expenses. Wouldn't want to see you get a fine. Uncle Sam is very unforgiving when it comes to his money." With that, the goth went back to staring at her tablet.

Dad was nearly speechless. "You hacked into my taxes?"

"Just a little sneak and peek. It's no big deal."

"It is to me! That's an invasion of privacy—"

"Privacy, that's cute." She started laughing.

"*Anyway*," RJ said, giving her a look, "we found your resume very impressive, Mr. Reynolds. I even watched some of your documentaries. The piece you did on the Bengal tiger was fantastic!"

"I watched them all," Kyle said. "My personal favorite is the Amazon adventure. Who does all that great post-production?"

"I'm pretty much a one-man show," Dad said, settling down but still eyeing Raven mistrustfully. "It's a big job, but I like to have total control over the final product. All I need is some funding, a camera, a laptop, and I'm good to go."

"Perfect," said Kyle. He sent a quick smirk to RJ.

"So here's what I'm thinking... The two of us should do a little documentary together. You're mainstream respectability, I'm alternative media. We combine your filmography brilliance with my crazy voice, your global television connections with my radio contacts, and we'd be totally unstoppable. I think we have the opportunity to do something really meaningful, maybe even change the course of history—from right here in Alaska."

Dad looked doubtful. "What did you have in mind?"

RJ paused. "Let me ask you this: you care about making the world a better place for our children, don't you?"

"Of course I do," Dad retorted.

"Then join me in exposing the Northern Lights government facility and their deathray! Your daughter hit it on the nose! We need to show the world what's really going on in that place. If we allow them to continue their experiments, who knows where it could lead. A thousand years of global domination the likes of which this planet has never seen! Well, not on my watch, pal! I want to squash evil like a fist full of grapes. Gaaah!" He demonstrated with his empty hand. "Oh, we are entering a dark, dark age, Mr. Reynolds. Do you want that hanging over your head? Do you want to look back at this day, this moment, and say, *Darn, I wish I would have done something when I had the chance?*"

Dad just looked at him.

"Information is power, Chase." RJ pressed him. "*You* know that. We need to slip in somehow and film what they're doing in there! Expose the rats for who they truly are. Sunlight *is* the best disinfectant, ya know."

Dad snorted. "It's my understanding that Northern Lights has more security than a supermax prison."

"And they say they've got nothing to hide," Raven murmured. "Ha!"

"That's what I said," I added.

"I hear what you're saying," Dad continued, barely covering his scoff, "and I admire your dedication, but I'm not convinced there is anything going on in that place worth getting so worked up about. A deathray? Come on. Sounds a little sci-fi to me. Maybe they *are* simply studying the aurora borealis."

RJ sat back in his chair for a moment, clearly gathering his energy for round two. He smoothed down his sandy-blond hair, took a few sips of coffee.

"Yeah, well, what if you're wrong? I'm not willing to take that chance. I'm asking you to sneak into Northern Lights with me. There has to be a way to get in. We gotta film the whole thing. The grounds, the antenna field, the facility. With you as the host of our documentary, the people and the mainstream media will listen. You have the credibility—"

"No way."

"Fine, then I'll be the host, but you've got to put your stamp on this, Chase. Think about your daughter. Do it for the children!"

"Give me a break."

"You gonna let these people get away with this? Come on, partner, whaddya say? I know you're a thrill seeker. This will be the thrill of a lifetime. Think about it, Reynolds! You've filmed everything from great whites to grizzly bears. You want to go after some serious big game? Then let's get in there and find out what the federal government is hiding! Booyah!"

"You're a lunatic," my dad said, half serious, half in jest.

"No, Mr. Reynolds. I'm an American!" RJ declared, and the way he said it gave me chills.

"I'm not as brave as you seem to think I am," said Dad. "A grizzly can only maul you. A great white can only bite you in half. The United States government is a whole different class of predator."

"Dad, I think I know how we can get in," I spoke up. "Northern Lights' website said they *do* allow a few exclusive tours every year. Famous documentary filmmaker bringing his daughter to see the place? You know they'd let us in. Certainly, the great Chase Reynolds could talk his way in for a tour. That would be good PR for them."

"You sound like your mother."

"Hmm, not a bad angle, Gabby, nicely done," said RJ, nodding. "I could pretend I'm a relative or something. I like this!"

I grinned at him. "See, Dad? Play it up that your kid is fascinated by the aurora borealis. Tell them I have posters all over my room—that I want to be an astronomer someday! Big shot like you? It would look suspicious if they refused, don't you think? We can do this!"

"We? What we?"

"You need me, I'm the kid! I'm your excuse to get in there. I'll bet some of the scientists on staff are already your fans. Celebrity VIP wanting to show his adorable little daughter all the cool sciencey stuff? C'mon, they're geeks and you're the rad Adventure King of Cool! They'll eat it up!"

"Laying it on thick, are we?" he drawled.

Dad was shaking his head, but I could see in his eyes that he was liking the idea more and more. Mom would have said that the adrenalin junkie in him was waking up.

I had my fingers crossed under the table. I could tell he was seriously thinking about it.

"C'mon, Dad, please!"

"Don't forget the bigger picture here, Reynolds. Together, we can warn the world about what these psychopaths are doing up there. If they're the ones causing the riots, let's shut the place down! We gotta do this for the future of this great country and the world! We the People, brother! Smells like a Pulitzer to me!"

I don't know what the tipping point was for Dad, but he muttered a curse word, still shaking his head, finished his bottle of fancy imported beer, then leaned back in his chair like a gambler at a casino about to bet all his chips on the roulette wheel. "I have a feeling I'm going to regret this, but we've got a couple of spare days, and since we're already here, what the heck. Let's give it a whirl and see what happens. But Hopper, I'm warning you, if I end up in federal prison over this, I'm going to kick your butt up and down the cell block."

RJ clapped his hands together and shouted, "Yes!"

The hippie high-fived us.

The goth just sat there brooding.

And I bounced with excitement in my seat.

The adventure was on!

Chapter 7
A Family Affair

As I said, my dad can schmooze anyone.

I don't know who all he talked to or what strings he pulled, but it turned out that the head science geek of Northern Lights—whoever it was—must have been a Chase Reynolds fan, because after a heavy dose of charm on Dad's part, we got permission to have our tour the very next day.

Mom would have wrung my neck if she knew what we were up to, and probably strangled Dad, too. Not that I could blame her. Still, it was for an important cause. Listening to RJ, you'd think the fate of all of human existence was on the line.

Feasibly, it was.

We met up in Dad's hotel room bright and early for a lengthy prep session. We were expected at the facility by noon, and since it was a five-hour drive to get there, it was a scramble to gather everything we'd need before we had to hit the road. We wanted everything in place before we left the room.

"Ow! You're pulling my skin again, Raven!" I shouted and

twisted as she taped a second wire to my back. "You're about as gentle as my dentist. How much longer?"

"Just hold still, little urchin. I'm almost done."

Between my dad's and RJ's equipment, thankfully, we had enough mics that all three of us would be able to record everything we heard.

As for video, Dad had some tiny cameras that he often sticks on unsuspecting wildlife after knocking them out with a tranquilizer gun. It's his trademark *Animal-Cam*, as he calls it.

So Raven repurposed three of them, giving my dad a hidden sport-coat-cam at about chest height, me one inside the large bow that the not-so-friendly goth techie had practically glued to my head earlier, and RJ a totally awesome hat-cam.

The cameras had their own internal microphones, too, so we figured we had every angle covered. But no matter how much you prepare, it's extremely risky wearing a secret wire to a meeting. People have gotten in big trouble doing such things.

Now if we can just manage not to get caught, I thought as Kyle burst into the room with a shopping bag in his hand and a big smile on his face.

"All right, boss man, I got everything you need!" He slammed the door shut behind him, laughing. "Thick glasses, fake beard, a cane, yellow food coloring for the choppers, and ta-da...gray hair dye."

"Come to Papa!" RJ said with a big hearty laugh as he popped up off the edge of the bed, grabbed the items, and disappeared into the bathroom. I heard the sink turn on as he began the process of transforming himself into an old man— Chase Reynolds, Senior, to be exact.

When he emerged twenty minutes later, we all busted out laughing at the striking transformation. He had even dyed his eyebrows. With a stooped posture and corn-colored teeth, he looked ancient.

"How do I look there, young folks?" He tried to alter his speech to sound forty years older; however, that famous croaky voice of his was hard to disguise. "Am I grizzled enough for ya, you young hooligans?"

"You look perfect, Grandpa," I said sweetly.

"Really great, Pops," my dad said. Raven couldn't help herself and went over to mess with his beard. "However, you're not allowed to talk. Not a word! If one of them were to recognize your voice, we're toast."

"Ha, funny," said Kyle. "Haven't you noticed the dude can't keep his mouth closed for more than five seconds?"

"I can, too!" RJ retorted in his normal voice as he pushed Raven's hands away from his face. "It's good. Leave it alone, Gilk. This isn't the first time I've been in disguise."

Raven pouted and went back to fiddling with Dad's coat-cam.

"Well, let's hope you don't have any regular listeners in there," I added.

RJ snorted. "I doubt it."

After all the technical issues were ironed out, we spent a bit of time rehearsing short scripts—answers to questions we expected to be asked. In particular, we needed to develop a backstory for Grandpa Reynolds. We didn't want to get tripped up on some minor detail, like where he lived or what his job was before he retired.

And right before we finally left the room, Kyle and Raven were given specific instructions that if the mission went horribly wrong, and it was at all possible to extract me from the facility, they were to take me to the airport and send me back to my mom in San Francisco immediately. They both promised.

So, a little before seven, we all went down to the parking garage where Kyle presented our groovy transportation.

Literally!

He slid open the side door of a flame-painted van that looked like it just rolled out of a sitcom from the seventies. "Gabby, you're with me and Raven in the back. Chase, here are the keys—you're driving, bud. RJ, park it in the passenger seat. Here we go, guys."

I climbed into the back and flopped down on one of the chairs. It was cushy and comfortable and swiveled all the way around. It didn't resemble anything I would think of as a car seat. In fact, it looked like someone had mounted a living room recliner to the floor. And there were two pieces of rope for a seatbelt.

I couldn't help but marvel at all the thick blue carpeting everywhere. It was on the floor, the ceiling, the walls, the chairs, the inside of the doors, the dashboard, and the steering wheel. It was as though a shaggy mold had spread throughout the entire cabin—slowly, over the decades—until it eventually covered every square inch of the interior. I giggled at the vision of the five of us arriving at Northern Lights covered in the stuff. Blue's not my favorite color. Why couldn't the carpet be purple?

I picked up the ends of the ropes and loosely tied them around my waist. "Is this thing safe?" I asked Kyle.

"Oh, she's sound, all right. Had her since I was a teen. I leave the little beauty with my parents and only get to drive her when I'm in town." Kyle snuggled down into the recliner next to mine. He kicked off his shoes, leaned his head back, and closed his eyes. "Welcome to the lap of counterculture, antiestablishment luxury. Isn't she something? Ahhh..."

"She's something all right," I mumbled.

As dad pulled the funky old jalopy out of the hotel parking lot, I watched Raven flip open a hidden compartment in the couch along the sidewall. Inside was a tool bag and all of the surveillance equipment she would need on her end during the operation. She opened up two laptops, slipped on some headphones, and began running her final equipment checks.

At some point, while we were cruising on Highway 3, she shouted above the noise of the engine, "Speak! Say something! The three of you...anything! And don't stop until I tell you to! I need to adjust the audio levels!"

Suddenly, assuming everything I was about to say would be recorded, I felt self-conscious, all locked up, and I didn't know what to say. Everybody seemed a little tongue-tied for a short moment.

Leave it to RJ Hopper to break the silence and start singing "America the Beautiful."

"O beautiful for spacious skies, for amber waves of grain..." He wasn't half bad considering he had an amphibian permanently stuck in his throat.

My dad joined in next and the two men half sang, half shouted the second line together. "For purple mountain majesties, above the fruited plain!" They sounded like two dudes who might have spent too long at a Fourth of July party.

But when Kyle joined in on the third line, even though he wasn't wired and could have just sat there mute, all of our jaws dropped at the rich, expressive tones that came out of that scrawny chest. He sounded like an opera singer. "America! America! God shed his grace on thee—"

All singing stopped.

We looked over at him, flabbergasted. He just shrugged with modesty. "I've had a few singing lessons."

Oh what the heck. I truly hate my singing voice, but I just couldn't resist. "And crown thy good with brotherhood, from sea to shining sea!"

We didn't stop there. We followed up with a lively performance of "My Country 'Tis of Thee." And for our final act, we hit a home run with a heartfelt rendition of "God Bless America."

I didn't care if it was cheesy. The three American classics seemed appropriate considering we were about to go into battle for her.

The old songs energized me. At that moment, I felt completely resolved to take on the challenges ahead, whatever they might be.

Before the last few bars, I turned to look at Raven, wondering if she was going to tell us that it was okay to stop. I noticed something different about her face. She was smiling, and her eyes looked a little misty.

I got the feeling the vampire-looking techie had finished her audio checks a few verses ago and was simply enjoying the ballads.

Music soothes the savage beast, so they say.

Maybe there was an actual beating heart in that cold chest of hers. And perhaps it was filled with affection for the red, white, and blue.

I know mine was.

# # #

For most of the drive, I stared out the side window, buried in my thoughts. The region was desolate. We would go for long stretches without seeing another car or any evidence at all that humans were ever there before us.

The wind was blowing from the north the whole time, as though it were trying to push us back to Anchorage, keep us away from danger.

We ignored Mother Nature's warning and eventually arrived at the main entrance of the Northern Lights government installation. The building was a nondescript block of cement with very few windows. The original architect was clearly not concerned with giving the place a warm, inviting feel. It was all business.

The tall chain-link fence topped with razor wire reminded me of a prison. Signs announcing NO TRESPASSING surrounded us everywhere. At least there weren't armed guards waiting for us.

Seeing the building, and the lengths they went to here in order to keep people out, made my heart race with nervous energy.

My dad read the sign hanging on the gate aloud as he pulled

up to the call box. "'No visitors allowed. Photography strictly prohibited.' I guess some rules were meant to be broken, eh? Last chance if anyone wants to bail. We all have to be in this together. If not, I'll turn around right now."

"Are you kidding me?" RJ exclaimed as he slammed his fist into the blue fur that covered the dashboard. "Grrrr! I didn't come all this way to tuck tail and run."

"Oh, I'm in. No backing out here," said Kyle.

"Ditto," echoed Raven.

Admittedly, I was nervous. Everyone turned and looked at me, the youngest member of the crew. I think I surprised them with my steadfast resolve when I said, "Let's roll!"

"Attagirl," said my dad as he lowered the driver's-side window and pressed the call button. Cool as a cucumber.

"Who's there? Is this thing on?" a male voice squeaked. He sounded like a kid.

"Um, Chase Reynolds. Here for my tour. And I hear ya loud and clear, good buddy."

"Oh, ahem, Mr. Reynolds." The voice suddenly shifted four octaves lower. "Er, we've been expecting you. Welcome to Northern Lights. We'll be right with you."

Dad looked around the van at us with a befuddled expression. He undid his seatbelt and shifted around a little.

"Please remain in your vehicle, sir. Do not exit the, er, groove-mobile, or whatever that is. We're sending security down to escort you to the building."

"I have my daughter and my dad with me. It was cleared."

"Yes, yes, I know." The boy voice had returned and it sounded annoyed.

81

How odd.

"No problem. Whatever you want," my dad said, trying to come off as pleasant and cooperative. Then he raised the window so they couldn't hear us. Obviously they were watching our every move. "That was strange. Who was that? Raven, did we get that exchange? Are the cameras on? The mics hot?"

She nodded. "Affirmative. All electronics are on continuous feed for the entire operation. I got it."

"Good! RJ, slowly pan your hat-cam around. We need to get some footage of the outside of this place. It's really creepy, huh?"

RJ casually turned his head from side to side. Then he looked directly at me. "Point that bow-cam in my direction, Gabby. I want to record something for the folks."

Raven told me earlier that whatever direction my nose is pointing, so is the camera. Therefore, it was simple to line up the shot. I did as RJ requested just as he began to speak.

"Ladies and gentleman, it's me, your humble radio host, RJ Hopper. As you can see, I'm in disguise. My team and I are sitting in a van right now outside the Northern Lights facility in The Middle of Nowhere, Alaska. The very same facility where our corrupt government claims it studies the aurora borealis. The very same facility where I believe they house a deathray the likes of which this planet has never seen!

"We are about to risk everything here today to expose what truly goes on inside these gates. We figured out a way to get in. We go willingly despite the danger, because if we don't bring down these tyrannical evildoers, what do we really have left to live for, anyway? Slavery? I would rather die on my feet than live on my knees, baby!"

"Here they come," I whispered, seeing a black vehicle approaching over RJ's shoulder.

RJ lowered his voice. "So, let me remind you, ladies and gentleman, of what Thomas Jefferson once wrote to James Madison: 'I prefer the tumult of liberty to the quiet of servitude.' I hope this doesn't get ugly, but it might. Regardless, it is with my hero Thomas Jefferson's words ringing in my ears that I enter this fight."

Ending his grim intro with a flourish, he stopped talking and turned back around.

The guy was such a pro.

Whether we find anything evil or not in there, I thought, *this documentary is gonna rock.*

It was *so* going viral.

Then a large black SUV with heavily tinted windows pulled up to the other side of the gate and stopped. It was impossible to see who was inside.

Whoever it was, they sat there with the engine running for what seemed like an eternity. Eventually the front door swung open.

"This," Dad murmured, "is the craziest thing I've ever done in my life, and that's saying something. Let's just play it safe in there, guys. If you can't make it happen, don't even try. You hear me, RJ?"

"I hear ya. Good luck, people."

I gulped.

A guy in a black suit got out and started walking toward the control box on the other side of the fence. He sauntered like the bad guy in a video game. He was tall and thick and wearing dark sunglasses. His shiny bald head kind of reminded me of a bullet.

He punched in an overly long code on the console, a loud buzzer sounded, and the formidable barrier slowly descended into the ground. He then came over to the van and rapped on the window.

Dad rolled it down. "Hey, there," he said calmly.

"Sir, I'm here to escort you and your two guests up to the facility."

"Yay!" I said, trying to dispel some of the tension with the cute-kid routine. "I'm so excited! We learned all about the aurora borealis in school!"

Barely a reaction.

Bullethead removed his sunglasses and stared at me. I looked directly into his cold, dead eyes. That guy was seriously creepy.

He slipped his sunglasses back on and turned back to Dad. "There are five of you. We only have clearance for three visitors."

"Oh, yeah, those two are staying out here. They are totally jet-lagged. Just flew in last night."

"Gonna catch some Z's, pal," Kyle chimed in, sliding down in his recliner.

Raven had already stretched out on the couch, headphones on, pretending to be jamming out to her tunes.

After a long couple of seconds of assessing the situation, Bullethead yanked the handle and swung the door all the way outward. "Unauthorized vehicles are not allowed beyond this point. I will need one of you two in the back to pull the van over to that gravel patch and wait for the tour to end. If the three of you will please come with me."

"Cool. *No problemo*," my dad said. "Hey, Pops, be careful getting out. It's a little higher than my car. Pumpkin, help your grandpa, won't you?"

"Sure, Dad," I said sweetly. My heart was pounding so hard I felt like it was shaking the van. I made a show of assisting "Grandpa." RJ leaned on his cane and we all started toward the black SUV. I couldn't tell for sure if Bullethead was buying it, but I thought he was.

We got into the other vehicle as all the layers of security slid back into place, locking us in with no escape.

Through the chain-link fence, I saw Kyle drive the van to the designated spot and kill the engine. The whole scheme was starting to seem really dangerous to me, but it was too late to turn back now.

Bullethead drove us to the side of the building and into an underground parking garage. Once inside, the three of us got out and were greeted by a pretty blond scientist in a white lab coat.

"I'm Dr. Ambry. Welcome to our facility. It's nice to have you with us," she said. "I'll be showing you around today. Right this way, please." She pointed to an opened entry door.

I thought for sure she'd be making cow eyes at Dad, just like all women did, more or less, but instead, she looked bothered, as though she would rather be back in her laboratory smashing atoms or accelerating particles or whatever it was that she did there. Anything but showing us around.

Bullethead stayed in the SUV, eyeing us suspiciously as we followed Dr. Ambry through the metal door and into the belly of the beast.

Chapter 8
K-Mack in Kontrol!

"A-are you sure this is a good idea, sir?" Dr. Figgs asked as he nervously wiped his brow. He was staring at a bank of monitors alongside his thirteen-year-old superior.

"Of course I'm sure!" Kelvin snapped back, taking his eyes off his guests for the first time since they had arrived. "How suspicious would it look if we refused a celebrity of Chase Reynolds's stature a simple tour? Think about it. We need to buy some more time, anyway."

"I suppose you're right."

"I always am. Haven't you figured that out yet? They won't see anything we don't intend for them to see, so calm down," he ordered. "Look at you, you're sweating like a pig. Get it together, old man. You're going to have to go down there soon and perform. And stop touching everything with your...your wetness. Gross!"

Kelvin watched as the red-faced Dr. Figgs clasped his hands behind his back, stood up straight, and elevated his chin. Clearly an attempt to maintain his pride in the face of the boy's constant ridicule.

Kelvin turned back to the screens, wishing he were alone.

"Because ya know, Dr. K-Mack, sir, it would be a huge tragedy to ruin everything we've worked for, *I've worked for*, for all these years, because you were on some...some reckless power trip." Dr. Figgs's voice was trembling as if he were about to cry. "*You*, they would give a slap on the wrist and a reassignment. *Me*, I'd end up in an eight-by-ten cell in some supermax prison. I'd never see the sky again."

"That's not going to happen." Kelvin shook his head in disgust. When the time was right, he had every intention of frying the old man's brain, too, just like the rest of them. But he couldn't just yet. He still needed him.

It was nearly impossible to operate the world's largest antenna field all by himself. Not to mention, the other eggheads looked up to the man like he was some sort of a rockstar.

It was a prudent move on Kelvin's part, keeping Dr. Figgs close and in a position of authority. The guy's status among the rank and file was invaluable, and it was the only reason he was allowed *into* Kelvin's ultra-modern, ultra-cool, ultra-spectacular penthouse control room in the first place.

None of the other pinheads were even permitted on the top two floors, let alone within the walls of the nerve center of the entire operation.

The room from which I will eventually rule the world!

They watched in silence for a great while until Dr. Figgs spoke up. "Does the old guy look familiar to you? I feel like I know him from somewhere."

"Hmm? Let me see." Kelvin squinted, pretending to take a closer look. "Nope! Maybe you two hunted and gathered together back in the Pleistocene era. Brought down a woolly mammoth."

"Sir!"

"Pshaw, I don't know! He looks like every other old geezer on the planet to me."

Dr. Figgs frowned. "Remember, you wouldn't be here if it weren't for me," he muttered under his breath.

"Relax, Marty! You know I make fun of everybody. It's not just you."

Kelvin grinned. The truth was, he did have at least a *little* respect for the man—mostly for his vision.

They had similar theories on what the Northern Lights facility could truly be used for: mind control on a massive scale.

Behind the scenes, Dr. Figgs and his followers had been working in secret for decades with no major breakthroughs. Even though their mathematical models said mind control was possible, they simply weren't smart enough to make it happen on a large scale.

Eventually, Dr. Figgs had heard about a young weapons designer working with DARPA who could very well be the perfect mastermind for the operation. Someone who had the brainpower to work out the wrinkles that had halted progress for the past several years. He had secretly contacted the Wünderkind, who had been eager to join the cause.

For K-Mack, it was a simple matter of getting assigned to the facility. DARPA salivated at the suggestion that Kelvin would use his superior intellect to design for them the biggest, baddest, weather weapon the world had ever seen.

The Northern Lights facility had been covertly studying weather manipulation for years, so it was the logical home base for his research. Of course, the military assured Kelvin that his weather weapon would never actually be used. It would act as a deterrent to the Unites States' enemies. Kind of like the atomic bomb. Well, aside from that whole Hiroshima and Nagasaki thing...

Not five minutes after setting foot on Alaskan soil, Kelvin had staged a successful overthrow of the facility, locked up any opposing scientists, and assumed the kingpin position as their leader.

Nobody outside the facility had any idea yet what had happened. The rest of the government thought it was business as usual at the Northern Lights research lab, including Kelvin's NSA spy-geek dad.

K-Mack had to admit that a weather weapon would have been fun, and he did dabble in it from time to time, to keep up appearances. But mind control was so much cooler and, let's face it, way more effective toward achieving his own supervillain goals.

Everything was going as planned—better than planned, in fact—and Kelvin had no intention of losing ground over a silly celebrity tour of the facility.

About thirty minutes into the visit, he and Figgs watched as Dr. Ambry took their guests' picture standing with a group of scientists—his scientists. A publicity shot, a souvenir if you will, for Mr. Reynolds to show his scores of adoring fans. Proof that nothing bad was happening in the land of the midnight sun.

"So far, so good," Figgs said, sounding a little calmer. His perspiration was down to a trickle. "They seem to be buying our ruse."

"I told you. I got this covered. They'll be out of here before you know it. Now shush, I can't hear what they're saying. And don't you have somewhere you're supposed to be? I think your stomach is grumbling. Hmm?"

"Oh, yeah, gotcha," Figgs said with a wink. He hobbled from the room, leaving Kelvin to watch the monitors in peace.

Finally.

There was more to Kelvin's reasoning, of course, as to why he had allowed the three Reynolds family members to tour the facility. He didn't tell Dr. Figgs or any of the other scientists what was on his mind.

Truth was, Chase Reynolds had media connections that might be useful when the time came to go public. He knew it was inevitable. It was, after all, part of his plan. And the man was so good at what he did.

So Kelvin let him come for a tour mostly to check *him* out. Only the timing wasn't right to confront the Adventure King just yet. It was still too early. They needed more time. Experiments in the United States were going great, but they were far from taking the operation global. Perhaps another three to six months.

Kelvin watched the foursome head down the fifth-floor hallway to the Observation Lounge, where they would be served lunch. That would conclude their tour, then they'd would be on their way.

As he stared at Chase Reynolds, he couldn't help but notice

that the guy oozed cool. Like, he didn't even have to *try*. K-Mack watched his every move. Dang, but everybody knew the ladies loved that guy, with his laid-back California style and surfer-dude hair. Kelvin tried to assume the man's relaxed posture, attempted to imitate his smile—his confident attitude.

It was as foreign to K-Mack's skin and bones as if he were trying to stand on his head. Maybe if he studied him closely he could pick up just one or two superslick moves that might impress the ladies. Not that getting a girlfriend mattered to Kelvin...much.

After all, his idol, Tesla, never had one.

He had to admit, though, the daughter *was* kind of cute. She must have taken ballet or something because she glided along behind her dad as graceful as a swan as they entered the observatory. That girl probably never tripped over her own feet like he did.

They were about to see the most impressive thing at the Northern Lights facility.

Well, except for *him*, of course, he thought as he flipped up the collar on the leather jacket he barely ever took off.

K-Mack's mouth twisted into a crooked smile as the three visitors walked over to the wall of windows and gazed out in awe at his personal geek heaven.

# # #

"Whoa, would ya look at that," Dad said.

"Holy ga-moley," Grandpa breathed.

Deathray or not, I had to admit the display was impressive. I slowly turned my head from side to side so my secret bow-cam could pick up everything. But no video was going to compare to seeing the metal-monster live.

Antennas as far as the eye could see were laid out on a flat piece of land in a perfect geometric grid. There had to be hundreds of them. Tall poles with rods sticking out from the center like giant umbrellas. Wires with orange spheres connected everything into a giant, industrial-looking spider's web.

But instead of a creepy spider in the middle, there was one lone black antenna, thicker and at least three times taller than the rest. Taller than any cell phone tower I had ever seen. A long, man-made finger reaching for the heavens.

At the moment, the finger was bent at an angle, pointing slightly to the south. Probably where the beam was focused and aimed—the barrel of the giant deathray gun.

If it truly was some sort of a gargantuan weapon, I felt sorry for whomever it was pointed at just then.

Suddenly I noticed goose bumps on my arms. "Is that thing on? Like, right now?" I blurted out.

"It's always on, young lady."

I turned my head to see who was speaking—an old man wearing a white lab coat.

He must have entered the room while we had our backs turned. "The ionosphere never sleeps, my dear. There are always secrets to be learned. Hello, everyone! I'm Dr. Martin Figgs, the senior researcher here at the facility.

"I've been here for thirty-eight years this past spring," he said, giving us a welcome speech that sounded awfully rehearsed. "Many of our scientists live in Fairbanks—your wonderful tour guide, Dr. Ambry, included. But I choose to live right here in the residential quarters. So I just wanted to welcome you to our facility...and my home."

He clapped his hands together and put on a big broad smile. It looked fake. "You are our very special guests today. So! Anyone hungry? I'm starving. We can eat lunch over here, at the table with the best view. Come! Dr. Ambry, will you join us?"

"It would be my pleasure, sir."

I was suspicious of the guy immediately. He was pouring it on thick, trying *way* too hard. And he was a bad actor.

There was something off about him. There was something off about the whole place.

I could tell we had only toured a small portion of the facility, and everywhere we went I felt like we were being herded and watched. Not to mention, where were all the people? I had thought the place would be buzzing with activity.

The five of us sat at a rectangular table with one end pushed up against the window. He was right: every seat had a great view of the antenna field.

We talked in a friendly manner for a while as two ladies served us a basic cafeteria lunch—turkey sandwiches, potato chips, and ginger ale. They didn't say much, or *anything*, rather. They were like two zombies dropping food and drinks off at the table.

"She's beautiful, isn't she?" Dr. Figgs said at length, staring out the window pensively. His eyes were glassy, as though he were staring at an exquisite piece of art and not something that looked like a mass grave for 1950s' television antennas. I expected to see Godzilla ripping through the wires at any moment.

"It's amazing, sir," my dad spoke up. I knew he was lying. The great nature lover would scoff at such a destruction of the rugged landscape. "And really, thanks again, you guys, for allowing us to visit on such short notice. It means a lot to my kid."

"No problem," said Dr. Ambry.

"It's our pleasure," said Dr. Figgs, looking my way. If he could have reached my cheek from where he sat, I got the feeling he would have pinched it. He directed his gaze back outside and said, "I've known her for so long, I feel like she's family. She has her own little quirky personality."

"And what's her personality like?" I asked. The guy was starting to annoy me.

"Oh, she's moody sometimes, sweet others. She can be gentle and kind or wickedly spicy. It depends on her settings, the temperature outside, how charged the air is, the barometric pressure, who's at the controls. It all affects her performance."

"The large antenna in the middle is impressive," Grandpa offered.

"We call that one Big Bertha."

"After the World War I howitzer gun?" asked Grandpa. "Odd nickname. Unless... Well, gee, is this also some sort of a weapon, doctor?"

Nicely done, RJ. Smooth.

I turned my nose and therefore my camera directly at Dr. Figgs. I noticed my dad casually adjusting his coat-cam, as well.

We were ready for any accidental confessions from the

brainy nincompoop.

Dr. Figgs immediately backpedaled. "N-no, of course not. Not at all. It's just a nickname! Um, *Bertha* in the Old English means *bright*. She is a spire of light, a beacon of hope, in an otherwise dreary world. That's all!"

"Hope for what, exactly?" I asked, keeping the pressure on.

He took a brief moment to collect his thoughts and wipe the sweat from his shiny forehead on a napkin. "One of the things we study with the antenna field is the weather and natural disasters. We hope to get so good at predicting these events that no one will ever have to die again in a flood, a tsunami, or a hurricane. That's what I mean by hope. It's a lofty goal, for sure, but you know, over eighteen hundred people, good people, died in Hurricane Katrina alone. Senseless loss. That's unacceptable to our dedicated team of scientists. If we can save lives, then all the effort and expense is worth it."

"Interesting," my dad said. "What else do you guys do with that thing?"

"Oh, well, we *are* a Navy installation, after all. So we have an entire department on the first floor that uses Big Bertha to communicate with submarines and military ships all over the globe. Goes on all day long."

"That's funny," I said. "I don't recall seeing any sailors or anyone wearing Navy blues downstairs."

"They're around." Dr. Figgs's face was reddening like a ripe apple.

If we could keep the pressure on, this old guy might actually snap. I was feeling optimistic and aggressive.

"Why can't they just send a text?" I said innocently. "Seems

95

like a lot to go through just to transmit a message. I mean, come on, I can text my mom all the way in San Fran and she'll get the message in seconds. Simple as can be. Well, provided the stupid towers weren't busted."

"Sure, we could send a cellular transmission if the target is close to land, but with Bertha, we can communicate with any vessel, anywhere on the planet. A battleship in the middle of the Pacific. An icebreaker in Antarctica. A submarine eight-hundred feet below the surface. Try doing that with a cell phone. We aren't dependent on the towers, and besides, there's very little danger of our Navy messages being intercepted by America's enemies. It's easy to intercept a text message. Our government does it all the time—to, er, terrorists. We don't want the bad guys doing it to us, now, do we?"

Dr. Figgs was hanging in there.

He hadn't slipped up yet. But I kept on pushing because frankly, I'd had enough of overeducated, smug smarties for one day and was feeling my teenaged-girl attitude welling up.

"How exactly does that thing work?" I demanded.

Dr. Figgs took a sip of his drink. "Well...it's all so technical; I wouldn't want to bore you and your family with a long-winded scientific explanation about electromagnetic frequencies. It probably wouldn't make much sense to you, anyway."

"Try me!" I shot back. "I'm a pretty smart kid. Been on the honor roll since kindergarten. I can take it."

I saw blotchy hives pop out on his neck. I wondered if he had much contact with kids, spending so much time at the facility. I could tell he was intimidated and rattled.

Good!

"Well, if you insist." He pointed out the window with a trembling hand. "We use the antenna field to generate specific wavelengths of energy. All that oomph then gets concentrated, focused, and released by Big Bertha into the ionosphere. We can either pulse the energy out or release it continuously. It changes the effect. Of course, we only deal with nonionizing forms of radiation, so it's perfectly safe. It's not like that thing can be cranked up to shoot gamma rays." He chuckled nervously, but got no reaction from us.

Just stares.

"Ah, that would take an entirely different type of setup. And *would* be dangerous. We then use very sophisticated instruments—fluxgate magnetometer, induction magnetometer, digisonde—to measure the effects our little bundle of energy had on the atmosphere. We coordinate with atmospheric scientists, climatologists, and meteorologists, and develop models of weather prediction. It's all very sophisticated and quite harmless, I can assure you."

He kept harping on how harmless it all was, like a prisoner who repeatedly says he's innocent. I knew he was hiding something—something big. I could just tell.

So I dug deeper.

As the words were coming out of my mouth, I hoped that my dad wasn't getting mad at me for being so straightforward. Our time at the facility was almost up, and I wanted answers.

"I saw on this one website that you guys can control the weather," I said bluntly.

"Oh, that's the stuff of science fiction movies and conspiracy theory radio talk show hosts!" Dr. Figgs said with a wave of the hand. "Just a bunch of hooey."

"Oh really? Well, then what about dolphins and whales? Could the energy shot from Big Bertha affect their echolocation?"

"I don't see how."

"What about a human? If a person got hit with the beam, could it affect them?"

"Well, we are very careful to keep our beam focused on the sky."

"But what if it did?" I slammed my cup down. "Would they do all kinds of odd things? Maybe violent things? Perhaps break storefront windows, get into fights, riot?"

"I need to go to the bathroom!" Grandpa shouted over me, breaking my heated line of questioning. "Would you help me, Gabby? My legs are feeling stiff and all jellylike from the stairs."

"Sure, Grandpa," I said with one last stern look at Dr. Figgs.

He looked dazed and slightly battered, like a boxer relieved to hear the final bell.

I got up, walked over to RJ, and helped him out of his chair.

"It's just down the hall on the left, dear," Dr. Ambry directed.

"Thanks."

Grandpa and I hobbled over to the doorway. RJ excitedly whispered congratulations to me for my efforts. Behind us, Dad hurried to lighten the mood by telling the scientists one of his most exciting adventure stories: the time he nearly got eaten by a komodo dragon in Indonesia. Dr. Figgs looked relieved at the diversion.

It was too bad.

We had come so close to getting the old guy to crack. But in the end, he had held his ground and gave us nothing. That meant we had no choice.

It was time to take an even greater risk.

Chapter 9
Two Plus Two Equals Five

"You got six, seven minutes max," RJ whispered as I held the men's room door open for him. "Don't get caught. Like your dad said, no unnecessary risks."

I felt a chill run down my spine, but I nodded as I let the bathroom door close.

I went and leaned against the opposite wall as if I was waiting for him. I shoved my hands into my pockets.

I was sure I was being watched even before I spotted the camera halfway down the hall.

What to do. What to do.

I felt paralyzed. I lost at least a minute just standing there. Then I noticed something: the stairwell door was right next to the girls' bathroom.

"Grandpa, I have to go, too. Wait for me right out here when you're done. Okay?"

I heard a muffled response. It sounded like it came from inside the wall. *Huh?* I had no time to wonder why.

I walked toward the restroom, then instead of opening its door, I grabbed the stairwell handle and stepped through. I hoped whoever was watching fell for the illusion.

The stairwell was deserted and quiet. The intensity of what I was doing hit me as soon as the door closed.

I was excited and motivated and determined—oh and let's face it, *terrified*, all at the same time. Thankfully, there weren't any surveillance cameras in the stairwell.

I went downstairs as fast as I could. Took the steps three or four at a time and quickly arrived at the fourth-floor entrance. My heart was pounding as I opened the door ever so slightly. Hearing nothing, I poked my head out and stole a quick glance. The lights were off, but I could still see that nothing was happening on the fourth floor.

Pulling my head back, I let the door quietly close and moved on.

It was the same on the third floor and then the second—all quiet. We had seen the entire first floor during our tour, so I decided to head back up the stairwell.

On the way upstairs, my sneakers were squeaking so loudly I had to walk up on my tiptoes, ballet style, just to keep them quiet.

My calves were burning by the time I got back to the fifth floor. I glanced at my watch. "Oh, what the heck," I mumbled, and bolted up another flight to the sixth floor.

Unfortunately, it was the same there—quiet, dim, and empty.

With each floor I checked, the thought that something sinister was emanating from this place, some sort of invisible wave energy that could cause riots in distant cities, seemed sillier and sillier. It all looked pretty normal.

I was almost ready to conclude the whole mission was a dud. We had risked being sent to Guantanamo Bay for no reason. Dr. Figgs and his associates might be nerds, but evildoers bent on disrupting the entire planet with mind control and weather modification? Eh, I don't know.

For the first time all afternoon, I was starting to have doubts.

I glanced at my watch again. Perhaps I could squeeze in one more floor. Old men do take a ridiculously long time in the bathroom.

So do teenaged girls, for that matter. I figured I could spare a little time before anyone got suspicious.

I darted up the stairs to the seventh floor.

Perhaps getting a little too comfortable, I carelessly whipped the door open, fully expecting to see yet another empty hallway.

To my surprise, the lights were on and I heard people talking somewhere. I let go of the door handle and spun to the side, out of the line of sight.

Although I couldn't make out their words, I continued to hear them talking as the door slowly crept shut. It seemed to be taking forever to close. And just before it did, cutting off all connection with the seventh floor, I heard a distant, blood-curdling scream.

My heart leaped into my throat as the door finally clicked shut, casting me into the relative silence of the stairwell once again.

I covered my mouth and slid down the cinderblock wall

until I was in a crouched position. I hugged my knees and instinctively made myself as small as possible.

I stayed there for a moment trying to rationalize what I had heard.

It didn't take long for me to start doubting my own ears. The longer I sat there, the more I was able to convince myself that it was only someone sliding a chair, or more likely, a heavy desk across the floor.

It only *sounded* like a scream. It wasn't *really* a scream.

But what if it was?

We would be leaving any minute to head back to Anchorage. And aside from the bumbling Dr. Figgs *appearing* suspicious, we had no real proof of anything deceitful going on at the facility. We needed some hard evidence. This could be the break we'd been hoping for all along.

Hunkered down in the stairwell, feeling more than ever like I just wanted to run away and never look back, I decided that I wouldn't be able to live with myself if I didn't at least *try* to find out who or what had made that horrible sound.

As I stood up, I comforted myself with the thought that I could always fall back on the dumb-lost-kid routine if I got caught.

But first there was something I had to do.

I walked the few strides over to the fire extinguisher. It was eye level, so I could just make out my reflection in the glass casing. With my bow-cam pointed straight ahead, I began to speak.

"Hi, Raven. Hi, Kyle. It's me, Gabby. Oh, obviously! You can see me. Sorry, I'm really nervous right now. I don't know if you were able to pick up that scream—at least I think it was a scream—pretty sure it was. And it wasn't a surprised scream or a happy scream; it was more of a terrified or an I'm-in-pain scream. Anyway, bottom line, *someone screamed* right here on the seventh floor, and I'm gonna go check it out. I just wanted you guys to know where I was and what I was doing before I go ahead and do it. Just in case, ya know, this goes badly. Well, okay, here goes. Wish me luck." I waved at my ghostlike reflection and turned around.

Unfortunately, I was unable to hear my two accomplices back in the van yelling at my face in their monitor. For even though Raven and Kyle knew the system was only rigged with one-way communication, it didn't stop them from shouting at me anyway, I found out later. Kind of like when people yell at the television or a movie screen.

"Gabby, run!" Raven had yelled.

"Get out of there! Hide!" Kyle had pleaded.

But how could I have possibly known that in the few short minutes that I was running around in the stairwell, the entire operation had been compromised and that we were totally busted?

What Kyle and Raven knew—that I obviously didn't—was that Grandpa Reynolds had just been apprehended on the first floor after falling forty feet down an air vent.

He had crashed right through the ceiling and landed smack in the middle of the reception area.

Bullethead was right there and charged the dazed radio host.

In the ensuing struggle, RJ's beard fell off, but his hat

miraculously stayed on, thus giving Raven and Kyle a front-row seat to all the mayhem.

Their boss had put up a good fight, but in the end, he had lost.

I had no idea that RJ Hopper, with his true identity revealed, was being marched into the elevator at the exact same moment that I had opened the seventh floor door for the second time and stepped across the threshold.

With how quickly things unfolded over the next few minutes, I'm not sure the outcome would have been any different if I *had* known.

Nonetheless, I noticed that the voices were coming from a room down the hall to the left, so I scurried in the opposite direction. I cringed when I passed under the surveillance camera, but pressed on.

I made a left turn down another hallway and began pulling on door handles. I wanted some cover, away from that ever-present eye in the sky. I could only hope that my snooping had gone unnoticed. It seemed unlikely, but I was already in so deep, there was no turning back.

Most of the doors were locked, but when I found one that was open, I ducked inside with only a little hesitation.

The room was dark, the shades pulled tight. The smell of rubbing alcohol stung my nose.

I felt along the wall and flipped a switch. The fluorescent lights slowly flickered to life.

I had happened upon some sort of freaky exam room. I saw an old dentist's chair with brown leather straps for the waist, chest, wrists, and ankles. They were laid open, waiting for the next patient to sit down and be restrained—or worse.

I moved my head around slowly to make sure the camera picked up every creepy horror-film object.

There were two long electrodes plugged into an ancient machine, a mouth guard attached to a circular metal head clamp, a row of syringes, vials, gloves, goggles, and a white lab coat slung over the back of a wheelchair.

"What is this place?" I asked Raven and Kyle, not expecting an answer. It just made me feel better to think I wasn't alone.

I picked up one of the vials. It was filled with a clear liquid. The label read SODIUM PENTOTHAL. Whatever it was, it didn't sound good.

I was starting to feel claustrophobic. The air was so heavy it was nauseating, hard to breathe. I had to get out of there.

I turned around to leave and saw a folder on the counter with REEDUCATION PROTOCOL written across the front in a long diagonal.

Is that another way of saying mind control?

I opened the folder. My brain was too rattled at that point to comprehend anything on the pages inside. It just looked like a checklist with lots of numbers, settings, and steps to be followed.

I made sure to get it on film, but then I put the folder back exactly where I had found it.

Oh, I was getting in deep, but this was way too important. The world needed to know!

When I stepped back out into the hall, nerves rattled, I jumped at the sound of another scream. This time it was much louder and closer. I thought it was a woman, and she sounded absolutely bonkers. Then I heard a rhythmic banging.

I inched my way toward the disturbing sounds despite every fiber of my being telling me to run in the opposite direction. I was terrified after stepping into Frankenstein's laboratory and I didn't want to end up being his next experiment, but I've never been very good at just leaving things alone.

I bolstered my courage and pressed on.

I quickly came to a fastened set of double doors. The sign above read RESIDENTIAL G-BLOCK. I heard more screaming as I walked under the sign and pushed my way through the doors.

All up and down the hallway were carts and bins and beds on wheels.

The residents of this hall were not living here willingly.

Gazing through a pane of rectangular glass in the first door to my left, I saw a man sleeping on the floor.

I went across the hall and peered into another room. I saw a woman sitting cross-legged on the bed. She looked spacey as she idly yanked out her hair, one strand at a time. Her scalp was red, scabby, and raw. I noticed she had no eyebrows. I ducked out of the way before she saw me watching.

In the next room there was a large, muscular man sitting on the floor. He was propped up against a padded wall. The poor guy was fully restrained. His arms were pulled tight across his chest by a straitjacket and his ankles were shackled together. The man's rugged face was contorted into an inhuman expression of fury.

I looked away in dismay and moved on.

The next room contained the screamer. I saw a woman wearing a helmet repeatedly smacking her head against the wall. And just as I was watching, she let out another frightful shriek.

What have they done to these people?

I felt like I might throw up. I knew I had to get back downstairs, but this little prison was so horrible, and those people were in such need of help, I couldn't leave.

That's when I heard a gentle tapping and saw a woman's face pressed up against the glass a few doors down.

I hesitantly walked toward her room. She didn't smile or anything, just watched me come over to the window.

She looked a mess, though not as bad as the others, like she was strong or hadn't had too much "reeducation," but she still seemed pretty downtrodden.

She opened her mouth and started exhaling on the glass. I noticed her lower lip was split in several places. There was a scab the size of a grape near the corner. She must have fought hard against whoever put her in here.

Once the glass was fogged, she used her finger to write me a message. She even had the wherewithal to write backward so the letters appeared normal on my side. She slowly scratched out: *I'm CIA. Help!*

"I hope you're getting this, guys," I mumbled as she finished. "This woman's in the CIA!"

She wiped away the message and looked at me with pleading, soulful eyes.

"What do you want me to do?" I begged.

She held her hand up to her ear and pretended to be talking on the phone.

"I can't. All the towers have been down for days."

Next she made a hand gesture as though she were putting a key into a lock.

I briefly looked around but didn't see any keys. When I shook my head, she started gently thumping her forehead against the back of the door in frustration.

There was something about the woman that just broke my heart and made me *have* to help her. She didn't seem so far gone, not like the others. I felt I could still save her. "Don't lose hope! I'll get you out of there!"

I tried to forcibly yank the door open. I twisted and pulled with all my might, but it was secure.

The situation looked bleak.

That does it!

I looked down the hallway for anything heavy. I grabbed a nearby wooden stand. It was the kind that hospitals use to set meals on for their patients to eat in bed.

"Get back!" I shouted and hoisted it up over my shoulder.

The CIA agent backed into the corner, gave me the double thumbs-up, and smiled at me with her bruised, painfully swollen lips.

The stand was bulky and heavy, but at that moment, I had so much adrenaline coursing through my veins, it felt as light as a baseball bat. I swung it over and over at the formidable barrier.

I didn't care how much noise I was making at that point. She needed to be freed; they all did. This was so wrong!

After a while, the glass was shot through with cracks in every direction, but it would not fall away no matter how many times I hit it. It was ridiculously strong. I swung and I swung until I was exhausted, then the tray table broke. It hit the tile floor with a loud crash.

I was sure the whole building could hear the racket.

The smashing had certainly attracted the attention of the other prisoners. All up and down the hallway, I could see their faces pressed against the glass windows of their cells. They were shouting and banging. It was getting extremely loud in the G-Block.

"Shhh! All of you! I'm doing the best I can!" I uselessly waved my arms to try to quiet them. They only got louder. The residents had become frantic.

Way down at the other end of the hall, there was another set of double doors. I froze as Bullethead stepped through them and started speed-walking toward me.

"Halt!" he shouted. "Stay right there, young lady! This is a restricted area! You're going to have to come with me!"

I started backing away.

"Easy. I'm not going to hurt you."

Unless I wanted to end up in one of those cells, I had to get out of there.

I took one final look at the CIA agent. She was wildly attempting to kick out the glass from her side of the door, her blond hair flying every which way.

I turned and ran from that hallway, ignoring all the pleas, cries, and screams of its captives.

Chapter 10
A Diabolical Dance

Bullethead was gaining ground as he chased me down the hall. He seemed inhumanly fast.

But I was pretty fast, too.

I ripped open the stairwell door and recklessly made my way to the fifth floor and back to the observatory.

I knew in my gut that I wasn't going to get away from him. I was caught.

"*Daaaaddy!*" My scream echoed down the fifth-floor hallway. I was almost there.

"Dad! Help!" I burst into the observation room. "This freak's after me! And there are people upstairs—"

Nobody was in the room. The table was littered with what remained of lunch, but everyone was gone.

Within seconds, Bullethead appeared in the doorway and stopped.

I turned, not sure how I was going to defend myself, but to my surprise, he did not enter the room.

"Oh, you're here, sir," he said stopping short. "I'll just go assist with the detainees." He closed the door.

Huh?

"Ahem!"

I whipped around. That was when I first laid eyes on the Dork of Doom.

A geeky kid with zits, he stood on the opposite side of the room, which was why I hadn't seen him at first. He was leaning against a support column, hands in pockets, head cocked to the side, trying to look tough or cool or something. I got the feeling that he had been working on that pose for a while before I had stepped into the room.

Kind of embarrassing.

"So," he drawled, "you've seen the seventh-floor, umm, residents?"

I ignored his awkwardness.

"Have you seen them, too?" I asked in a whisper, at the time not having a clue who he was or what he was doing there.

"I have. It's just awful. Isn't it? Tsk, tsk, tsk."

He was obviously mocking my concern.

"Have you seen my father?" I asked pointedly. "He's a tall blond guy. Chase Reynolds? He's on TV. Maybe you've heard of him?"

He tilted his head to the other side, eying me the same way one would study a lab rat. "Oh, I've heard of him."

"Well, do you know where he is?"

"I might."

"What is going on here?" I asked suspiciously. "Does one of your parents work in the building or something? Is that guard your dad?"

"Ha, that would be a switcheroo."

"Would you *please* just tell me where my father is?"

He folded his arms across his chest. "I'm afraid he's been detained."

"Detained? Why?"

"Hmm. Do you really need to ask, Miss Reynolds?"

"How do you know my name?"

"I know *everything*."

"Okay, that's enough talking in circles. *Where* is my dad?" I demanded, taking a few paces toward the scrawny geek.

Unless he secretly knew karate, I was sure I could kick the snot out of him.

He stumbled backward, slipping and almost falling.

"Th-that's close enough!" I noticed he was clutching a small black gadget in his hand—something between a cell phone and a remote control. "Your father is fine. We just need to ask him a few questions."

Terror gripped me. "Like those people upstairs? Oh, no you don't!" I shouted, stopping a few feet in front of him. "Who are you?"

He took a few more strides away, placing one of the support columns partially between us. He peeked out from the side. "I'm the new management. The new head honcho." He snapped his fingers and pointed at me. "I'm...K-Mack."

There was a long, uncomfortable pause.

I stared at him, baffled.

He dropped his hand unceremoniously down to his side.

"You've got to be kidding," I finally said. "You expect me to believe that you're in charge? You're, like, eleven."

"Eleven?" His face turned red. "I'm thirteen, and I happen to have an IQ of one-seventy."

Could this boy actually be in charge of the Northern Lights facility? He wasn't even five feet tall. He was as skinny as a toothpick. "There's no way! Who would follow your orders, except maybe some oversized, brainless rent-a-cop who *has* to listen to you 'cause that's his job?"

"He has a brain, sort of, and yes, I am in charge."

"Fine, then tell me what's going on, right now, or I'm going to beat it out of you!"

"Ah, ah, ah... I wouldn't do that if I were you." He ducked further behind the column and held his contraption at the ready. "Don't make me use this."

"What? Are you going to give me a 'reeducation,' too? Turn me into a drooling birdbrain?"

"If I must."

"Okay, fine," I said backing off. I needed a moment to gather myself before I throttled the little dweeb.

"All this yelling is not going to get us anywhere, Gabriella. Perhaps we should chat for a while. Have you had dessert?"

"I want to see my father!"

"Then you had better be nice to me."

He strolled over to an intercom console by the door. "Brenda! Bring us some of that delicious apple pie. Two extra-large slices." He turned toward me. "Do you like yours à la mode? That means with ice cream."

"I know what it means. Whatever." I walked over to the window and stared at the deathray while he finished giving

114

Brenda her instructions.

I had to admit, assuming he *was* in charge, Kelvin had all the power. I was trapped, with no sign of any help on the way. I could have tried to run again, but he'd just sic Bullethead on me.

The only thing I had in my favor was the hidden camera and microphone.

I made up my mind to use it to my full advantage. It was time to take a gentler approach.

"K-Mack," I said without taking my eyes off the antenna field, "I'm not stupid. I know you guys aren't going to just let me walk out of here after what I saw upstairs."

He took his time but eventually walked over to me, uncomfortably close, and gazed out at Big Bertha, as well. He smelled of tuna and cheap cologne.

"I won't lie to you, Gabriella. It's true, we can't let you go and blab. You could ruin everything for us."

"I won't tell—"

"Yes, you will," he snapped back. "No girl can ever keep her mouth shut."

We stood in silence for a moment. It was obvious that Kelvin had been hurt by someone in the past for that very reason. I wasn't surprised, considering how bizarre and socially awkward he was. He must have been picked on ruthlessly ever since he was a little kid, too.

"What's going to happen to me? To the three of us?" I asked.

"You really want to know?"

"Yeah, you can tell me."

"The guy with the big mouth is with Dr. Hitzig right now. He's receiving a low level, single-phased memory wipe. It takes about thirty minutes. Your dad is next. And then, I'm afraid, sweetheart, you go in after them. I'll eventually send my guys out to nab the two in the van. They'll go last. After some recovery time, we'll drop you off in Anchorage—you won't remember a thing about what you've seen here. In fact, the whole past week will be foggy." He turned toward me. "So, just think, we only have about an hour to get to know each other, kitten. Purrrr!"

Oh, gross!

I quickly looked back outside. "Does the memory wipe hurt?"

"Eh, I don't know. Maybe a little. I've never thought to ask. Cool thing is, what does it matter? You won't remember, anyway." He snickered.

He was right in a twisted sort of way. As terrifying as it sounded, I got at least a drop of comfort knowing that the repulsive boy standing next to me would be erased from my memory, as well.

"This is sick. You know that, don't you?"

"Well, you only have yourselves to blame. Coming in here with all your lies."

I didn't know what to say. "We were trying to get the inside scoop on what really goes on in here, that's all. There are so many rumors and mysteries that swirl about this place; we were trying to get a Chase Reynolds exclusive when we set it up. Fine, so we weren't being totally honest with you. But I am now."

"Because you have no choice." Kelvin stiffened his spine. "Humph!"

Just then the door to the observatory opened. "Your pie, Dr. Mackowsky," Brenda said flatly.

Mackowsky...? I didn't put it together at first, just glad for the interruption.

The cafeteria lady looked as dazed and lifeless as she had serving lunch earlier. "Anything else, Dr. Mackowsky?"

Kelvin walked over and grabbed the two heaped-up plates. "How many times do I have to tell you people, it's K-Mack!"

Brenda had no reaction and simply left the room.

It took a few moments, but then I realized why the boy's name sounded so familiar...

Dr. Mackowsky!

I had read his paper online a few days earlier! The one about turning the antenna field into a weapon. *He's a kid?*

It took me a minute to absorb it.

"Has Brenda been mind-wiped?" I whispered after the door had fully closed.

"Something like that," he shot back with a pout. He set the dessert down on the table and licked a glob of ice cream off his thumb. "You are in no position to be asking questions, anyway. I'm very angry with you." He stomped his foot. "How did you think you would get away with this? I am a bona fide genius, you know. I'm way smarter than you!"

"Yeah, well, I'm way cooler than you," I answered calmly.

He narrowed his eyes at me for a moment, then let out a sigh. "Oh, come on over. The ice cream is melting and the pie is getting cold. Your lies won't matter anymore once you're mind-wiped. Until then, we might as well just hang out. After all, cool girls always love supervillains, according to my comic books."

"Oh really?" I said dryly. "Wonder why."

"Duh, because supervillains are rich and powerful," he said.

"You don't know a whole lot about relationships, do you?"

The nerd blushed and looked away. "That's a nice bow in your hair, by the way."

"Thanks," I said blandly. "My friend Raven gave it to me."

I hesitantly walked over to the table, pushed a couple of empty plates aside, and sat down across from him.

I took a few nibbles, just to keep up appearances, but I was not interested in dessert.

I was interested in not getting mind-wiped. And figuring out how to escape.

"Okay, I've been honest with you," I said at length. "Now it's your turn. I know you guys claim to use this antenna field for peaceful purposes, but I'm having a hard time believing that story after what I saw upstairs. I read your paper, *Dr. Mackowsky*, on your theory about how this facility could be used for mind control. So, tell me: Are you the one behind the riots? You might as well go on and claim your bragging rights while you can if it's true, because I won't remember later anyway."

"Wait—you read my article? You? I don't suppose it made much sense to you. But I gotta say, that's kind of flattering." He giggled and shoved a giant spoonful of pie into his mouth. He took forever to finish chewing, but when he was done, he finally admitted the truth. "Yeah, Gabriella. Guilty as charged. It's all me, cupcake. A devastating, shock-and-awe, hide-the-children K-Mack Attack!"

For such a young supervillain, he definitely had the diabolical laugh down.

"Well, congratulations," I said sarcastically. I got up and paced, kind of freaked out all over again. I couldn't believe I was truly at the epicenter of all that had been going wrong in the world.

At least it wasn't our own leaders creating all the mayhem as RJ had thought.

It was just this insufferable genius.

But maybe I could get through to him.

I've always been pretty good with people. Besides, Kelvin obviously thought I was cute.

I rested my hands on the back of the chair and made sure my nose was pointed directly at Kelvin. I decided to give him the opportunity to do a little bragging for the camera. "How did you manage to get control of this facility?"

"Ah, it was a well-planned strike," he said, leaning back, gloating. "It wasn't very hard, actually—took all of about twenty minutes. I had people on the inside."

"Like Dr. Figgs?"

"Yeah, old Marty Farty and about a dozen others. But you should have seen me. I was lightning fast." He climbed up on his chair and acted out the part. "Like a king cobra. Hisssss! Whack! Whack! Down for the count!"

He was the strangest boy I had ever seen.

Somehow I guessed Bullethead had done most of the work.

The evil boy genius carefully got down from the chair and took his seat. "And anyone who didn't join us, well, you saw what happened to them. The United States government has no *idea* what we're doing with their little Tesla toy. They think it's business as usual up here in Alaska—just messing with the weather."

"So you guys actually *can* control the weather?"

"Well...more or less. The conspiracy nuts got that one right. Of course, it's hard to predict with any certainty what effects we'll have when we fire that baby up. There have been a few...accidents."

"Hurricane Katrina?"

"Actually, no. That was Mother Nature. Minor mishaps only—you know, a hurricane here, a few tornados there. That sort of thing. Oh, I'm sure I could perfect their techniques if I gave it my full attention, but I'm not really interested in the weather. It's mind control that gets me up in the morning. It takes a delicate hand, a sensitive touch." He blew on the tips of his fingers.

"How does it work?"

"So glad you asked! First, I stun the people with ELF waves. Then, at just the right moment, I throw in some pulsed microwaves, and voilà. I'm like Mozart on the piano, Neil Peart on the drums." He started banging away on the air drums. "Depending on the microwave frequency, I can turn people into anything from docile little sheep to crazed, angry barbarians. It's hilarious!" He giggled wildly then stopped drumming. "Of course some people are surprisingly immune to my little wavelength games. Not sure why. Maybe something to do with willpower. Most people are just such empty-headed couch potatoes, though, that they're easy to influence and control."

"But why are you doing this?" I cried.

"Because I can. Because I'm K-Mack the Awesome. That's why!"

"That can't be the reason. Just because you *can*?" I fired back. "Do you have any idea what you're doing to those people out there? You've turned the whole world to chaos!"

"Hey, if you had to live under the constant control of the CIA like I have, you'd appreciate a little chaos, too."

"Oh, I see. So, it's all about you!"

"Darned straight."

"And what if somebody you care about gets hurt in one of these riots? Family? Friends? Grandma? Come on, there's got to be someone out there you care about."

"Why?" he suddenly shouted. "Nobody cares about me!"

I struggled to understand what he had just admitted, and slowly, it dawned on me. "So that's what all this is, then. People have made fun of you in the past, misunderstood you, refused to be your friend. You feel like nobody cares about you, and this is your revenge."

Kelvin shifted uncomfortably in his chair. "Friends are for losers."

I had struck a nerve. It was written all over his face and in his body language. In a weird way, I felt sorry for him. Even though he wanted to mind-wipe me.

I sat down. "It must be really frustrating, Kelvin. Being able to understand and figure out so many things...but not people. So instead you just try to control them with this machine?"

"No matter how hard I try," he said in a low monotone, "people just don't make any sense to me. I don't know what they want. They're illogical. Unpredictable. I don't know how to make them like me."

"Oh, Kelvin. You can't *make* people like you. First you've got to like yourself."

"Huh?"

"See? I knew it. You're not a bad person."

"Oh yes, I am. I'm a-a supervillain!"

"No, you don't want to hurt anyone, Kelvin. You just figured this was a good way to get everyone's attention."

"You have no idea what you're talking about."

"Yeah, I do. You're lonely, so you're punishing the world."

"Whew, you are way off base!"

"Oh, really? Have you ever been to a baseball game?"

"Huh? No! Boring!"

"How 'bout a birthday party?"

"Thirteen of 'em," he shot back.

"Your own don't count. But were there any guests at your parties?"

"Well, my parents and their high-level clearance friends."

"Wow, sorry I missed those shindigs. Sounds like a blast. How about a museum?"

"Useless junk!"

"Have you ever snuck out of your house in the middle of the night and went running around in the woods with a bunch of friends? And then crawled back through your window just before the sun comes up, only to realize that your face hurts and your throat is hoarse from laughing so much?"

"You've done that?"

"Of course!" I threw my arms up. "Every kid has!"

"Huh. Sounds fun. But that wouldn't actually work for me, 'cause I have an RFID chip implanted in my ankle so my CIA handlers know exactly where I am at all times."

"That's ridiculously sad." I almost—*almost*—wanted to hug him, I felt so sorry for the dork. "Have you ever just been a kid without all this brainiac nonsense?"

Kelvin pondered the question for a while. "I went to the zoo once. I was about seven. My parents were in Europe and my aunt Ellen dropped by unannounced. She convinced my handlers to keep a respectful distance. It was like they didn't even exist for one whole, glorious afternoon. We ate funnel cake. It was fun."

"The zoo, eh? So you like animals?"

"A lot more than humans."

"So you know killer whales, right?"

"Sure, but they're actually dolphins."

I rolled my eyes. "I saw a group of them—"

"It's called a pod!"

"See, this is why people aren't going to like you! Stop being a know-it-all! Dude, social skills! Just be quiet and listen. Anyway, I was out on this research vessel at Glacier Bay a few days ago and we came upon a *pod* of killer whales. They were so amazing and beautiful. There was only one problem."

"What's that?"

"Four of them apparently got confused from all the extra energy and frequency waves and whatever else is coming out of Big Bertha. And they swam up onto land, accidentally got stranded. And died."

"Oh no!" He paled, looking genuinely horrified. "I did that?"

"Yeah," I said with my eyes cast down, feeling the pain of that day once again. "By the time we got there, only one was alive. His name was Lightning, but we couldn't save him. I watched him die."

Kelvin slumped against the table, looking dazed. "I

didn't...mean for that to happen. I've got nothing against the whales. Honestly!"

"Have you ever seen an animal take its last breath, Kelvin?" I asked softly.

"N-no."

"Well, I hope you never do, because it's sadder than you can imagine. What a waste."

We sat there in silence for a little while. Eventually Kelvin spoke up. "I feel kind of terrible about this. I never meant to harm any animals."

"Then turn off that machine. Stop doing this. It's in your hands to end all this craziness right now. If you did that, well, then that's the kind of guy I could be friends with."

"Really?"

"Yeah. Maybe we could even hang out. Like go to a movie sometime. Get a bite to eat."

"Like a date?"

"Well, no, not exactly. We're twelve and thirteen. Not a *date*."

"Hmm. Tempting, but I've come too far to stop now. Gabriella, I am not going back into that prison."

"What prison? What are you talking about?"

"I was identified as a prodigy when I was only two years old. Ever since then, my life has been a nightmare. All of my days are filled with training and work, work, work. It's all I do! They've been using my genius for their own selfish motives since I was practically in diapers. Not to mention, I'm constantly being watched. It's not right! It's like serving a life sentence."

I stared at him. He scowled back. "Don't look at me like

that. I don't want your pity. I'm not some sort of weakling. Far from it. I have more power than anyone else on this planet right now, even the president. Heck, even the head of the United Nations. And power is a rush!" He punched his fist into his palm. "Do you find power attractive, Gabby? 'Cause I'm just oozing with the stuff!"

"Okaaay," I said in a diplomatic tone, trying not to laugh in his face.

Thankfully, Brenda walked in just then with two mugs of coffee. She set them down and left.

"I had asked her to wait for a while and then bring us some coffee," Kelvin said with a shrug. "If you don't like coffee, that's fine, I'll drink it. I could get you something else if you want. Hot chocolate? Herbal tea? I think we have some fresh orange juice."

"See, Kelvin, you *can* be nice. You *can* be normal. That was very sweet of you. I'll drink the coffee, though. Thanks."

After a few sips and not a whole lot of talking, the building started to rumble.

"What the...? Earthquake!" I dove under the table in a panic.

Everyone in my hometown knows that if you can't get outside, that's what you do when the ground starts shaking. Either that or stand in the nearest doorway.

I watched K-Mack's chicken legs tremble as he laughed at me. "It's not an earthquake, Bow-Head. Gosh, living in San Francisco has made you paranoid. Take a look outside."

Frowning, I crawled out from under the table, dusted myself off, and went over to the window.

"Hey! How do you know where I live?" I demanded.

He smirked. "Please. *Big data* is my middle name. I'm

joking," he added at my look of confusion.

"Whatever." I shook my head at his whiz-kid prying and looked out the window.

The building continued to rumble until the giant antenna came to rest facing almost the exact opposite direction of where it had started.

"What is going on, K-Mack?"

Kelvin looked at his watch. "Oh wow. Time sure zooms along when you're having fun, doesn't it? Nearly thirty minutes have gone by already. Sheesh! We had a weather test scheduled. Slipped my mind. Keep watching. It's quite impressive when she bows out the ionosphere."

I turned back around, my mind reeling at the fact that thirty minutes had passed. My dad's memory was in great danger of being erased. The reeducation may have already started, for all I knew. I had to figure out a way to help him, and soon. I didn't think I could handle it if my own dad didn't remember me.

Nothing much happened with the antenna field for a while, then *whoosh!* The air seemed to ripple out from the center, as though someone had tossed a big rock into a still lake.

When the energy waves reached the clouds, they spread the fluffy whiteness out into a giant, undulating circle.

I stared up at it in amazement.

"Mmm, beautiful, isn't it?" Kelvin startled me by whispering in my ear.

He had snuck up behind me while I wasn't looking.

Sneaky little bugger. I nearly jumped out of my skin. I looked sideways at him, my lip curling in disgust.

"Don't be surprised if it's windy and rainy tonight. I find the rain so romantic, don't you?"

Gag!

"Is that it?" I asked while stepping to the side, trying to ignore his cringe-worthy flirting.

"Well, yeah! We're not exploding antimatter bombs here. So sorry to disappoint you."

"No, no, it was...pretty," I assured him cautiously, my mind running through different scenarios I could use to escape and save my dad.

I wanted out of there. Bad. Then, as if by magic, the opportunity presented itself.

"So what do you like to do, Gabriella?" He just insisted on keeping up his ridiculous flirtation. "Hobbies? You must like sports, 'cause you seem so...sporty."

"As a matter of fact, I do." A smile spread across my face as inspiration came to me.

He wasn't going to like it very much, but the way I figured, he had brought this on himself.

I counted off my three main activities. "Hmm, let's see. I've been doing freestyle dance since I was four, gymnastics since I was five, and ballet since I was six. I'm thinking about going out for cheerleading this year."

"Cheerleading? Wow!" Kelvin looked truly impressed. "You do move like a gazelle, you know that? Gabby the Gazelle is what I'm gonna call you from now on."

"Aw, that's cute." I gave him a dimpled smile and pretended to be flattered. Whatever charm I had inherited from my dad, it was time to put it to use.

"Can you show me some moves?"

"Well, sure! I was hoping you'd ask." I grabbed him by the shoulders and moved him back a few paces to just the right spot.

He looked thrilled that I had touched him.

Ick.

Although he was still holding his little electronic device, he made no threats against me as I forcibly pushed him backward. It seemed Kelvin Mackowsky was starting to trust me. "You stand over here. Okay?"

"Okay! How exciting." He clapped his hands. "Have you ever been in a show?"

"Tons of them."

"Like, you have a tutu and everything?"

"Pink, black, teal, and even one in faux leopard print."

"Wow."

"Okay, no more talking. I need to focus."

"Yes, ma'am!"

"I'll start with a round of double tours."

His eyes were nearly as big as his glasses, and I thought he might hyperventilate as I stood in fifth position, arms raised high, concentrating for a moment.

He watched in rapt fascination as I dropped my arms, did a slight plié, and leaped into the air.

I went high, spun around two times, and landed in the exact same position and in the exact same spot I had started in.

He clapped insanely. "Bravo, Gabby the Gazelle!"

I just smiled. With only a slight pause, I did it again. And then a third time. All the while I stared at a particularly big zit on Kelvin's forehead, using it as a fixed point of reference so as not to get dizzy.

He clasped his hands together and smiled from ear to ear at my performance. You would have thought it was Christmas morning. Poor thing. He looked truly happy for the first time all afternoon.

See, Kelvin, having a friend is not so bad.

But the good feelings wouldn't last long. After my fourth cycle, I paused for a moment and shifted my weight to my back foot.

"Sorry, Kelvin," I said, and truly meant it.

I felt bad for what I was about to do. But I had no choice. My dad's memory was at stake.

"For what?" he asked, just as the heel of my foot swung around like a battering ram and collided with the left side of his head.

I nailed him with a butterfly kick, square in the temple.

My friends and I had been practicing that move in the park for a while. I had never actually done it to a real person before. Sort of like a ballet move turned karate.

Poor K-Mack.

He dropped to the ground as I landed in a fighter stance, ready to inflict more pain, if need be. But there would be no more fighting.

The Dork of Doom was out cold.

His glasses and his gizmo had skidded across the floor. I wasn't exactly sure what the device did, but I knew it was trouble, so I smashed it under my foot and felt a satisfying crunch.

His glasses, I left alone. I didn't have the heart to break them, though I probably should have.

As Kelvin lay on the ground in a crumpled heap of nerd, I raced out of the observatory in search of my dad.

I only hoped I wasn't too late.

Chapter 11
The Good Doctor

Moments later, I burst out of the stairwell into the seventh-floor hallway. I spotted Bullethead sprawled facedown on the floor. My dad was standing over him, his fingers pressed to the unconscious guy's throat.

"Holy heck, Dad! Nice work!" I shouted as I ran toward him. "What did you do?"

"Nothing! He was escorting me to some office. Nobody will tell me what's going on! Only that they caught 'my father' snooping around and they needed to ask me some questions."

"Questions, huh?"

"Yeah. Then this dude just passed out for no reason! *Boom!* Crashed to the floor about a minute ago. I think he might've had a heart attack or something. He has no pulse!"

"Whoa! Like exactly a minute ago?"

"Yeah, why?"

"Um, never mind. Leave him, Dad. He's one of the bad guys. No time to explain. We have to find RJ and get out of here.

Everything we thought about this place is true, only it's much, much worse. Come on! I think RJ might be in this room over here."

"How could you possibly know that?" he exclaimed as he followed me down the hall. "Where are we going? And where have *you* been this whole time? I've been worried sick about you. They wouldn't let me see you!"

"I'll tell you later. Brace yourself, Dad. This could be ugly."

I whipped open the door to the reeducation room, and sure enough, there was RJ strapped to the chair. He looked unconscious, with his eyes rolled up into his head.

A man in a white lab coat was sitting beside him. I glimpsed DR. F. HITZIG M.D. monogrammed above his left pocket as he turned toward us and started yelling.

"Vhat is zis? Hilfe! Sicherheit!"

My dad got between me and Dr. Hitzig. "Look, man, we don't want any trouble, we just want our friend. So back off!"

The slick, red-haired doctor stood up with a sneer. "Ah, Herr Reynolds, I presume. You are but a few minutes early, *ja*? Pleaze vait outside. Sicherheit? Vear are you?"

"If you mean the guard, he's not coming," Dad shouted, and whipping out a canister of bear repellent, he sprayed it right in the guy's face. The doctor backed off, flailing.

"Ahhh! *Meine Augen! Meine Augen!*" He spun around a few times, crashed into the wall, but eventually ran from the room screaming his way down the corridor.

We let him pass.

I raced over to RJ and quickly ripped off all six straps, yanked out the bite guard, and unclamped the electrical pads from his forehead.

"This is *sick!*" my dad said in shock, covering his nose with his sleeve. "Did they do this to *you?*"

"No, Dad! Hey, stand over there and get some footage of me and RJ! This place is so evil."

"Good idea, Spud. But let's hurry. This pepper smell is awful." He lined up his coat-cam and held still. "You know what? I think they were bringing *me* up here for this...treatment!"

"You catch on fast, dude," I mumbled, trying hard not to breathe.

RJ was as groggy as if he had just drunk two bottles of cold medicine.

"I knew we were getting in over our heads," Dad mumbled. "Why did I ever let you talk me into this?"

"Dad, not now! RJ, can you hear me?" I smacked him on the cheek.

He turned to me slowly. His eyes weren't quite tracking right, and his tongue flopped out of the side of his mouth while drool ran down his cheek.

I thought he was going to say something, so I leaned in close, but all he did was start laughing. Then he reached up and gently cupped my face in his large hands.

"Mitta Potodo haaad," he slurred as he started pulling on my nose and squeezing my cheeks. It made him laugh even more.

I gently lowered his hands.

"Ooookay." I turned to my dad. "Um, I think I might need your help. He is so cuckoo right now. I hope this isn't permanent."

133

"Come on," Dad said grimly. "We better get him out of here."

The two of us helped RJ out of the chair and to his feet. He swayed back and forth as though he were on a boat out at sea.

Down the hall we went. We each had an arm draped over our shoulders. RJ's head flopped side to side and forward most of the time, so he was providing very little assistance.

Admittedly, Dad was taking the bulk of his weight, but the radio guy felt heavier than I would have guessed.

"This way! Follow the exit signs!" my dad urged as we blasted through the G-Block double doors.

I had no time to warn him that we had just entered a makeshift prison.

I noticed the inmates standing silently at their windows right away. They wore hollow expressions, like lost souls. I felt so guilty that I had been unable to help them earlier.

This place is going to haunt my nightmares.

It took my dad a few strides before he noticed them.

"What the—?" He stopped dead in his tracks. "Gabby, there are people in these rooms! Oh, man, they're all messed up."

"I know, Dad. I came through this way before. This is where they locked up all the folks who wouldn't go along with the takeover. They messed with their brains. I guess to keep them docile or something."

"Takeover? I see I missed some important details. This is so creepy. We've got to get them out!"

"There's no way! I already tried. The doors are locked and it's shatterproof glass. See that window? That was me. I bashed it with that knocked-over table a hundred times and it still didn't break. It's no use."

"Sheesh, Gabby! *You* did that?"

"I lost it trying to free the woman inside. She's a CIA agent, Dad. All that noise, it was my fault we got caught. I blew our cover. I just couldn't help it. We're already slowed down with RJ. If you ask me, the best thing we can do for them right now is to get out of here with our minds intact and go get help."

"We can't just leave them like this."

One of my dad's greatest virtues is that he's super compassionate. Seeing his fellow man being treated in such a despicable way had to be breaking his heart.

Like father, like daughter.

"Please, Dad, RJ's not getting any lighter! We need to keep moving. I don't want us to end up like them!"

His face hardened. "You're right. I never should've brought you into this place. I want you out of here, *now*. Let's move."

It wasn't easy to get going again. RJ seemed to grow heavier with every step we took down the hallway. My muscles were screaming, but in a twisted sort of way, the inmate's vacant expressions kept me going until we reached the other end of the hall.

"We'll send for help," I uttered to the last face I saw.

Then we went through a second set of double doors and were out of G-Block.

We hobbled another fifty feet down a quiet hallway to the emergency exit. Dad pushed open the door.

At last, air as refreshing as a cool lake on a hot summer's day blasted us in the face and filled our lungs. I felt instantly rejuvenated.

But still, you have no idea how hard it was to carry a deadweight like the mumbling, helpless RJ Hopper down all those flights of rickety metal stairs to the ground below. We simply took it one step at a time and did our best not to lose our balance.

About halfway down, I heard a crashing sound. "What was that?"

Dad squinted into the distance. "Looks like the cavalry's arrived."

It wasn't until I saw that old, junky van screeching to a halt at the bottom of the stairs that I realized that the crashing noise had been Kyle and Raven ramming through the gate to come and rescue us.

I never would've imagined I'd be so happy to see that old groove-mobile.

Kyle and Raven both jumped out and came running up the fire escape to help us.

"Oh, are we glad to see you guys," I mumbled as we shifted around, each grabbing a different limb.

I had RJ's right leg, Raven his left, and the two men each had an arm.

"We recorded everything," Kyle said. "Great job in there...Gabby the Gazelle."

I knew he was only teasing, trying to lighten the mood, but I cringed at the reminder of K-Mack's nickname for me.

In no time, we made it the rest of the way down and piled into the van.

RJ moaned and rolled over onto his belly when we set him down on the shaggy blue carpet. He started snoring almost instantly.

"He looks bad," Raven muttered.

"Let's get out of here," Dad said as we piled into the back.

"Do you think we should take him to a hospital?" Kyle asked while Raven began rolling the door shut.

"Would you just drive?" she yelled at him.

"Fine!" Kyle ran around to the driver's seat and started the van. It lurched into motion.

Raven immediately began fiddling with her equipment.

Dad and I sat down hard in the backseat, exhausted.

The first drop of rain hit the windshield with a *splat* just as we drove over the broken gate and tore off at top speed, leaving the grounds of the Northern Lights facility behind.

I watched nervously out the back window for a long time, scared to death that black vans—or black helicopters!—might appear at any moment, following us.

But none did.

Bit by bit, mile by mile, we seemed to be all right, in the clear.

We sat in silence, all probably trying to absorb everything that had just happened. I couldn't help brooding on all of those poor people trapped in their prison cells. Human experiments.

I wondered if K-Mack was still lying unconscious on the observatory floor.

At length, Dad asked, "Anyone want to explain to me what happened back there? I'm feeling out of the loop here."

We each took turns filling in the puzzle pieces of what had occurred from our own unique perspectives. I told him about my seventh-floor discoveries and the thirty-minute encounter I'd had with K-Mack, a.k.a. Dr. Kelvin Mackowsky. Dad laughed when I told him how I'd escaped.

"Oh, I knew all those years of dance would pay off! Wow! A butterfly kick? You make me so proud, Spud."

Kyle spoke next about what had happened to RJ after Bullethead had captured him. I felt a slight sense of relief when I learned that it was *RJ* who had blown the whole operation first, and not me.

What was he thinking climbing into the ventilation system?

Raven said little, only filling in the parts that Kyle had missed. All the while, she was tinkering with her equipment and what looked to me like the van's electrical system.

By the time Dad was up to speed, the rain was coming down hard.

"Can you see all right up there, my friend?" Dad asked Kyle.

"I'm okay. Just let me concentrate for a while. You guys talk."

"If you want to trade places at any time, let me know."

"Thanks. I will."

"Hey, I got it!" Raven burst out, her gaze fixed on the equipment.

"What?" I asked.

"The signal from RJ's hat-cam! It's back at Northern Lights. I was having the hardest time with all the interference in the air, but I tapped into the van's classic 102 whip antenna to boost the feed, and look!" She pointed at the monitor screen. "This is why I *love* old-school technology. Might not last for very long, but there it is. We're rollin' live!"

My dad and I went over to join Raven in front of the

monitor. Wherever RJ had left his hat, the live feed wasn't picking up much. All I saw was a countertop, a wall, and part of a file cabinet.

"Do you guys hear someone shouting on there?" my dad asked. "Turn it up, Raven."

As the volume increased, I distinctly heard the voice of the evil boy genius himself, coming from somewhere in the background.

"How could you let them go?"

"That's K-Mack, Dad," I volunteered.

"I figured," Dad muttered.

"Vhat would you have me do? I was blinded. Look at *meine Augen!*"

"That's no excuse! You should have done a little of this... Waaa! And a little of that... Hi-yah! It's all about confidence, power, and intimidation, Dr. Hitzig. Eee-yah!"

I rolled my eyes at the weakling's bravado so soon after being knocked out by a girl.

"Du kleiner Wicht! Ich werde dich umerziehen nächsten Mal!"

"Stop that! You remember the rule. No speaking German around me. You could be making fun of me and I wouldn't know it. What did you just say there?"

"All I zaid wuz how sorry I wuz to have let zem escape."

"That's more like it. Hey, look—the old man's hat."

We suddenly got an extreme close-up of Kelvin's face as he inspected RJ's hat.

We were far closer to that mug than any human should ever venture. I saw his eye had already turned black and blue from my kick, and his glasses sat bent and crooked on his pimply nose.

The picture jostled from place to place for a while and then went relatively still. Judging by the height and point of view, we could tell that Kelvin had just put the hat on his head. A cockeyed image of Dr. Hitzig slid sideways onto the screen. He was standing in his laboratory, right next to the torture device he had used on RJ.

It gave me the chills.

"I wish we would have smashed that thing," I said through gritted teeth.

"Auf Wiedersehen, Dr. Hitzig."

"Auf Wied—oh, er, goodbye to you, too, Dr. Mackowzky."

The image bobbed and zigged down the seventh-floor hallway.

"Oh, please don't go to the bathroom," I mumbled.

We all looked at each other in dread.

He got on the elevator instead.

"Whew," we collectively sighed.

Kelvin pushed the button for the thirteenth, the top floor.

The inside of the elevator was covered in mirrors, so there he was again, leaned up against the side rail, looking ridiculous in RJ's old-man fedora hat.

As the elevator jostled about, he took a few steps forward and gazed at his own reflection on the opposite wall. We watched as he touched his left eye and winced in pain. Then he sneered at himself. "How could you have been so stupid? She was only *pretending* to like you, you numskull. She's just like all the rest! Guess it really is just you and me against the world, my

140

friend," he said to his reflection.

He pulled the brim of the hat down to cover at least some of the bruise, scowling at himself. "There, that's better. Getting beat up by a girl. This hat doesn't look half bad. Kinda retro-vintage-hipster. Hey there, pretty dame." He blew a kiss, gawking as he practiced his flirting again.

"Ugh." I buried my face in my hands, having been on the receiving end of his "charm" before.

The elevator door opened, and Kelvin swaggered down another hall with his new hat tipped over one eye like an old-timey mobster. At length, he entered what had to be the command center for the entire facility.

It looked more like a place to blast off rockets than their cover stories of simply launching secret messages to submarines and innocently studying the weather.

We got to see an impressive wall of monitors as Kelvin scanned the screens running feeds from surveillance cameras throughout the facility. He was mumbling to himself all the while.

"What's he saying?" my dad asked.

"I can't tell. Oh, Dad, he's so strange. There's no telling what he might be griping about. Probably about me kicking him in the head. It made such a terrible noise when I connected. I'm glad I didn't give him a concussion."

"He deserves it," Raven muttered as she adjusted the settings, but we still couldn't make out what Kelvin was saying.

All of a sudden, he shrieked when he saw the broken entry gate. "Those jerks!"

Raven leaned in and started pointing and shouting at the

monitor. "Too bad, K-Mack, you spoiled brat! That's what you are! You're nothing but a rotten little reptile!"

Dad and I exchanged a surprised look at Raven's outburst.

She's been hanging out with RJ too much.

Over the next several minutes we got to see quite a bit of Dr. Mackowsky's control center. It all looked so high-tech and sophisticated; I was surprised *anyone* knew how to use all that equipment, let alone a teenage boy.

The room was overflowing with floor-to-ceiling computers, each covered in meters, knobs, buttons, switches, and levers. It almost seemed alive. Needles flicking, lights flashing, dials spinning.

After a while, Kelvin must have walked over to the window because we got another look at the antenna field, only from a higher vantage point. The rain shrouded the whole array in an ominous, milky haze.

Kelvin went over and sat down at a wooden desk. He kicked his feet up and grabbed a nearby children's toy.

"Really?" Dad asked flippantly. "So this is what little Dr. Doomsday does after a hard day of wreaking havoc on the planet? A puzzle game. Now I've seen it all."

We got bored silly watching his hands spin and twist and rotate the cube-shaped object. I took a break from all the "excitement" to peek through the oval window at the back corner of the van.

It was raining so hard I could barely make out the hills and trees in the distance. I pressed my nose against the bowl-shaped glass and squinted. As if the universe sensed my frustration, a bolt of lightning lit up the entire landscape.

I gasped when I saw a menacing cloud formation in the shape of Kelvin's face. It hovered above the tallest mountain, as though the boy genius were directing the forces of nature to do his bidding.

The puppet master in the sky.

I tried to convince myself it was only my imagination as I sat there nervously waiting for the next flash of lightning. A moment later, Mother Nature released another massive lightning bolt. And the face was gone.

I breathed a sigh of relief.

"He's done," said Raven.

I shook the image from my mind and went back over to her monitor to see Kelvin admiring his handiwork. All of the colors were now lined up properly.

"This hat is killing me," he muttered and whipped it off, throwing it to the floor. We watched the camera spin around like it was on the most violent teacup ride ever created. It was nauseating, actually. I looked away until I heard Kelvin shout, "What the—"

We watched as he got up from his chair and walked slowly toward the hat until he loomed over the camera. He bent down with a look of disbelief on his face.

"Uh-oh," Dad said.

The three of us held our breath, waiting to see what he'd do next.

"A camera!" he shouted. "Why, those sneaky little roaches!"

Suddenly, we had a full mug shot of the boy. He looked startled and confused. Then I watched as the dawning realization spread across his face—that not only had we recorded the whole visit, but we were watching him at that very moment.

"Ahhh!" he suddenly shouted, and crinkled up his face with a toddler's fury. A spray of saliva hit the lens. "Oh! I will get you for this! You hear me, Gabriella? My new best friend?! I hate you! You...*liar*!"

I moved back. Kelvin's rant was a little unnerving.

"Who do you people think you are?" the enraged boy screeched at the camera. "Well, let me tell you this. K-Mack will have his revenge! Ahhh!"

With that, we could only assume that he threw the hat again, because everything spun violently for several turns until we came to rest, staring at the motionless wall.

Within seconds, however, he was back and looking slightly calmer. He spoke directly to the camera.

"Okay. You idiots made your move. Now it's my turn. I'd like to dedicate my next number to my great 'friend,' my wonderful girlfriend, Gabriella Reynolds. This one's just for you, Gabby the Gazelle. Think I'll start with an earthquake in San Francisco... Enjoy!"

The sight of his bitter smirk was cut off with a *pop* and then the monitor went black. All communication with K-Mack had been cut off.

We sat there for a moment, speechless.

"An infant with a deathray," Raven spoke up. "Perfect!"

"What are we going to do?" I cried. "What about Mom? My friends?"

"I don't know, Gabby," Dad answered solemnly.

"Can he really do that?"

"Seems a little far-fetched, but after all I've seen today, I'm not so sure anymore."

"Well, we have to stop him! We have to tell somebody!"

"Like anyone's gonna believe us," Raven said.

"Dad?"

"Well... I could edit down the raw footage tonight and take it over to the police or the FBI as soon as it's ready. It won't be perfect, but at least they won't have to sift through hours of video to see the proof."

"Great. I'll help," I said, happy to have some direction.

"Raven, can I use your equipment tonight to get this done?" Dad asked.

"Of course," she answered hesitantly. "Just be real careful with it. With all the towers being offline, I've got no way to back up the footage onto the cloud, yet. You'll have the only copy. No mishaps, Chase, or we got nothing and this whole adventure was a waste."

"No problem," he said. "I got this."

A few miles up the road, Kyle pulled over onto the shoulder.

"Phew. That was some really intense driving. Mind taking over for a while, Chase? I'm exhausted."

"Not at all," he said, giving me a kiss on the forehead to try to ease the dread on my face.

Kyle practically crawled into the back and crashed on the floor next to RJ. He stretched out his legs and clasped his hands behind his head while Dad took the empty spot behind the wheel.

I tied myself into my chair with the makeshift seatbelt for the long drive we still had ahead of us.

By the time we hit Anchorage, the rain was coming down so

hard it was as if K-Mack had turned a fire hose on the city.

There was no way to know if the rain was just nature or a deliberate attack. But I guess that's the whole point of having a weather machine.

What do they call it in the spy movies again? I mused, searching my brain. *Oh yeah.* I remembered.

Plausible deniability.

Great.

But somehow, I knew it was Kelvin behind the storm.

Chapter 12
Breaking News

"Do you think RJ will be okay, Dad?" I asked as I peered out the window at downtown Anchorage early the next morning.

It had stopped raining sometime before dawn, but the sky was cloudy and didn't look in a particularly friendly mood.

"Not...sure," he drawled without taking his eyes off the computer screen. I wasn't convinced he even heard the question.

Kyle and Raven had decided to continue down the Kenai Peninsula despite the bad weather and drop RJ off with his parents in Homer. They planned on hopping a plane back to Juneau, where they would keep the radio show going by running old sound bites of RJ's best rants. There was apparently an endless supply of them.

No one had any idea how long it would be before the radio host was back to his old self again—if ever. The last I saw of him, he was mumbling something about blue cheese.

After the slow, slow drive through the storm back to Anchorage, Dad had been up all night editing video. He was adding subtitles whenever the audio got garbled, and narration to describe what was happening in real time. As soon as it was ready, we were going to take it to the authorities.

"Hey, would you get away from that window?" Dad suddenly scolded me. "They might see you! I'm not joking!"

"Being a little paranoid, don't you think?" I mumbled. I took one last look at the morning crowd shuffling off to work and let go of the curtain. "Kelvin has no idea where we're staying. For all he knows, we could be on a plane heading to Fiji right now."

"I wouldn't be so sure, Gabby. He has his ways. He knew you were from San Francisco, which is why he made that threat against your hometown. Plus the kid's obviously an expert hacker. He could have looked up my recent credit card purchases and found out where we're staying. Maybe even tapped right into the hotel's surveillance cameras. If so, then I bet he even knows what rooms we're staying in." He suddenly lowered his voice and glanced around. "He's probably listening to us right now through the sockets. RJ said they can do that. Maybe you should run the shower to drown out our voices."

"I'm not running the shower! That's just a silly waste of water. Geez, Dad, it sounds like you went from being a total skeptic to a complete conspiracy nut overnight."

"Can ya blame me? Fine, never mind about the water. But don't think for a second we're in the clear, because we're not."

"I suppose."

My dad was getting increasingly paranoid and I was growing ever more restless. I had barely slept a wink all night, and I couldn't seem to shake my nervous energy.

Earlier, I had paced back and forth between our two rooms

for what felt like hours. Then I tried practicing my gymnastics moves. I raced up and down the hall like a crazy person doing every manner of tumble I could think of until my foot crashed through the cheap wall and I nearly broke my neck.

Nothing is working.

I kicked my leg up onto the wall for like the millionth time and stretched out my hamstrings in a giant oversplit. I felt like I had drunk a hundred cups of coffee. Then I completed yet another sixty-second gymnastics tick tock challenge. It was useless; I couldn't seem to calm down.

Maybe Kelvin was running some strange microwave frequency over the city, making my dad paranoid and me a hyper spaz.

"Whoa, come look at this!" Dad called to me. "I got to the part where Dr. Hitzig is putting that metal thing on RJ's head. The bald security guard and a couple of goons just strapped him down in the chair."

"Oh no!" I said, and dropped out of my latest round of handstand push-ups.

We could only see the top half of RJ's head due to the positioning of his hat-cam, but he looked kind of loopy—not his normal spunky self.

"Dr. Hitzig must have given him a shot of that drug already," I said. "I can't remember what it was called, but I saw it in the reeducation lab."

"Sodium Pentothal. Yeah, he did, right in the neck. I watched it earlier when they were interrogating him."

"What is that stuff?"

"A strong sedative. Mostly just mellows ya out. However, it's also called 'truth serum' because people can't help but blab stuff when they're on it. They got RJ to admit who he really was. But the guy's tough. He didn't say much else. Even after a second shot to the other side of the neck."

I cringed at the thought of getting two shots in the neck and turned my attention back to RJ and Dr. Hitzig.

The doctor must have thrown the switch, because, on the video, RJ's eyes rolled up into his head and he thrashed around uncontrollably. It was hard to watch. I had to look away at several parts during the lengthy session.

As the treatment wound down, he resisted less and less, until he looked practically unconscious—more or less the way we had found him.

"That German doctor guy is horrid," I mumbled.

"Ugh! I was only a minute away from getting that treatment, Gabby. Do you realize that?" Dad was squinty eyed and rubbing his temples. His famous cool hair was looking all Albert Einstein. "That could have been me in there."

"And I was right behind *you*," I said, staring at his face. "Are you okay, Dad? You look exhausted."

"I think so. It's just...my head is pounding."

"Take a break! Lie down for a while. You haven't stopped working on this since last night."

"It's too important to stop now. Who knows what that little punk is planning to do to us all? Maybe he's already started. I'm almost finished, anyway. I just want to get a bit of that last part with Kelvin in the control center, do my final checks, and then render it complete. I need...maybe another hour, tops. Then you're coming with me to the police station. There's no way I'm leaving you here alone."

"With pleasure. But I'm going down to the lobby right now to get you some coffee. You look like you could use it. Then you're going to need to get yourself cleaned up. The great Chase Reynolds can't be showing his face at the police station looking like you do. Trust me on this one."

"Gabby, I don't want you leaving our rooms or at least our floor. You're a good daughter, offering to look after your old man like that, but I'm okay. Just stay here. It's safer that way."

"Dad! I'll be fine. I can't stay cooped up in here any longer. I'm going crazy. It's like I'm in jail again! I'll just run down to the lobby for a minute. Please? You know how slick I can be. I'll take the stairs and stay away from that fancy glass elevator."

He stopped and rubbed his eyes in exhaustion, letting out a sigh. "A coffee does sound kind of awesome right now. I guess if you just go to the lobby and come right back..."

"You want some aspirin, too? And a bagel?"

"You're sweet. There's money in my wallet. Thanks, hon, but tie your hair up before you go and put on a ball cap. *And* sunglasses!"

"What, like a disguise?"

"Just do it!"

"Okay. Whatever you say." I took a few quick strides and did a grand jeté clear across the hall and into my own room. Free!

# # #

The lobby was crowded.

I stayed back for a while and looked every which way for

151

Bullethead, Kelvin, or any of his thugs. I didn't see them anywhere, so I entered the main part of the lobby and started walking over to the little convenience store right inside the hotel. Nobody was paying any attention to me. That was good.

When I was almost through, I noticed a crowd of people gathered in the fireplace lounge area. It seemed kind of strange, because no one was talking. They were all just staring intently at a wall-mounted television. Several of the women had their hands covering their mouths and most of the men looked like their eyes were going to bug right out of their heads.

I took a slight detour to see what they were watching—the local news.

I sidled up behind an old woman with overly dyed hair and too much perfume, but she was short so I could easily see the TV over the top of her head.

"...all cell and now wireless communication appears to be down clear across the greater Anchorage area," the way-too-pretty female newscaster said. "In fact, this morning, for the first time all summer—and what a crazy summer it's been!—it appears to be a global issue. Let me repeat that: All cell phone communication and Wi-Fi is down across the entire planet! Yes, ladies and gentleman, it appears that we are all stuck using the old-fashioned landline until someone is able to figure out what is causing this. Now back to Mike Aleman for an update on our top stories."

That wasn't your top story? I thought in astonishment. *You mean it gets worse?*

"Thanks, Jane. If you're just joining us, brace yourselves, folks, it's a busy news day. The riots, which had quieted down, are back in at least twenty-three major American cities today, the hardest hit being Orlando, Baltimore, and Honolulu Hawaii, of all places! The president is considering declaring martial law to better protect all American citizens. Fortunately, aside from that wicked storm we had last night, there are no specific disturbances to report in Anchorage as of yet. We'll keep you posted on any developments throughout the day."

I slipped off my sunglasses and glanced at the faces of the people around me. Aside from looking worried, they all seemed fairly normal. I wasn't feeling entirely right myself, but I didn't feel the sudden urge to break a storefront window or anything.

Dad, admittedly, seemed a little off today.

"Now, on to the extraordinary amount of bad weather and seismic activity we are seeing all over the globe. Where to begin..." Rick Aleman was looking a little freaked out as he gestured to the animated weather map. "We have four tropical storms with the potential to turn into hurricanes in the Atlantic Ocean, all bearing down hard on the East Coast. They just popped up out of nowhere within the past few hours. Also, a major earthquake rocked central Chile this morning. It measured 7.3 on the Richter scale. Rumbles were felt as far north as Bogotá and as far east as Rio de Janeiro. No reports of any fatalities as of yet."

I was relieved that nothing was reported about California.

"Tsunami warnings have been issued for almost the entire western half of the Ring of Fire. That would include New Zealand, New Guinea, Philippines, Japan..."

"Oh, K-Mack," I whispered in dread, "what have you done?"

As if summoned by the sound of my voice, he suddenly

walked through the front door with Dr. Hitzig, Bullethead, and four other big, burly dudes in tow.

Dr. Hitzig was wheeling a suitcase that I could only assume contained the mind-wipe machine. Bullethead was looking seriously scary in his usual black suit and dark sunglasses. The goons were unnerving, as well, dressed in white hospital gear from head to toe.

What a motley crew.

I pushed my way forward, almost knocking the old lady over in my efforts to hide. I pulled the brim of my hat lower over my eyes.

With his long black duster coat billowing out behind him, Kelvin marched across the lobby and into the empty elevator.

I tried to think of something I could do to warn my dad—anything—but without my cell phone, and with the bad guys taking the elevator, I couldn't come up with a single way to reach him in time. Perhaps I could find a hotel courtesy phone...

Frozen in place, I watched the elevator doors glide together. But then, suddenly, two hands jutted out and stopped the doors from closing fully.

When the chrome doors parted, opening back up, K-Mack whipped off his shades and stared directly at me. I drew in my breath. I couldn't believe he had seen me. I felt the blood drain from my cheeks.

My dad was right!

He *did* have his ways.

A wicked smile spread across his nerdy face. He turned and said something to Bullethead.

I couldn't hear the exchange, but Bullethead remained

expressionless. I started inching my way away from the crowd as the people continued to stare in horror at the news program.

Kelvin blew me a kiss and then yanked the little black gizmo out of his coat pocket. The same one I had smashed under my foot only the day before. He must have fixed it somehow.

He dangled it back and forth in front of his face, teasing me, proving that he was superior. Then he started frantically tapping the thing with his finger.

Within seconds, Bullethead's eyes homed in on me. My jaw dropped, and that was the moment I fully realized that K-Mack was controlling his big, bald bodyguard with that device.

From the first time I had seen Bullethead in the parking lot at Northern Lights, I had noticed there was something very mechanical and unnatural about the towering man in black. And I knew now what made him that way.

Bullethead was some kind of super advanced cyborg *robot* thing. And he—or rather, *it*—was coming straight toward me.

At first Bullethead only walked off the elevator and motioned me over with a few flicks of his finger. But as I stepped out of the crowd and bolted for the front door, he kicked it into high gear and chased me right out into the street.

With my hat flying off in the sudden cool breeze, I wasn't so sure I could outrun him a second time.

Chapter 13
Battle of the Bullethead

"Hey! Watch it, kid!"

I crashed into a tall man with bushy hair but kept on sprinting down Fifth Avenue.

I glanced over my shoulder. "Sorry!" I yelled just as Bullethead barreled into the same stranger with all the force of a freight train. The poor guy went sprawling across the sidewalk—never knew what hit him.

One block down and Bullethead was right at my heels.

I considered screaming, but I figured most people would take the side of the nice man in the suit trying to apprehend the little criminal girl who probably just shoplifted from the local drugstore. Mom always says no one wants to get involved in anything anymore and that politicians actually have to make laws to *force* people to help others.

"Halt! You are being apprehended!"

I felt Bullethead's cold, ironlike fingers grasp my shoulders. I shrieked and made a hard left, directly into traffic, slipping from his clutches.

Breaks were slammed, curses yelled, and fists lifted out of car door windows. I ignored it all and just kept running full speed across the street and farther down Fifth Avenue.

The next time I glanced back, Bullethead was running across the top of a line of cars right down the middle of the street.

He was easily keeping pace with me as he dented hoods and roofs. He was making quite the spectacle of himself.

I came to a row of bikes lined up on the sidewalk. A large yellow banner read BICYCLE RENTALS. I hopped on the bike at the end, flicked up the kickstand, and tossed a twenty-dollar bill at the man heading my way with a clipboard. I assumed he was working there.

"I'll bring it back in one piece! I promise!" I yelled as I placed my foot on the pedal ready to shove off.

"But wait! You have to fill out the form!" he shouted. "What are you doing?"

"Sorry, gotta go!" I pushed down hard, just in time to miss being clobbered by Bullethead as he leaped off the closest car and crashed into the row of bicycles in a vicious attempt to tackle me. The long row toppled over like dominoes as I sped down the street.

I was able to create some distance as he struggled to get himself out from the pile of handlebars, tires, and chains.

I pedaled as fast as I could all the way to the end of Fifth Avenue and made a right into Elderberry Park. My dad and I had been to the park only two days earlier when we were doing touristy things. It wasn't very big, but it did provide access to the

Tony Knowles Coastal Trail—a long bike path that wraps around the city and then wanders for miles through the surrounding area.

"Try to keep up with me now, android," I mumbled angrily as I made a left onto the trail and headed downhill at lightning speed.

The route curved at first but then coursed almost perfectly straight, paralleling the water's edge.

I went all out for about half a mile before turning to check if I was still being followed. The path was clear for as far as I could see.

The bad weather was probably keeping people away. It was chilly and yucky out.

Breathing a small sigh of relief, I slowed up and downshifted several gears. My thighs couldn't take much more of the nonstop pedaling and needed a break.

No sooner had I pushed the lever than the chain started to make a loud clicking noise. I fiddled with the gear changer and it turned into a grinding sound. I tried pedaling backward, which only resulted in the chain popping off completely, and then I lost control, almost wiping out.

Dang it! Of all the dumb luck! Kelvin can build a robot and I can't even shift gears.

Another glance behind me and still no sign of Bullethead. It was eerily quiet, too. The only sound was the squawking of seagulls somewhere in the distance.

I flipped the bicycle upside down so it was resting on its handlebars and seat. The chain was tightly wedged between the sprocket and the frame. I struggled to free it.

And then I saw him.

Bullethead was way back on the trail, running hard with inhumanly long, bounding strides.

I yanked. I pulled. I spun the pedals frantically and finally dislodged the chain. I hooked it on to the first few teeth, and with shaky hands, forced the pedals forward, only to catch my finger in the gear.

"Ow!" It started to throb with pain right away, and the chain dangled loose again. I turned to look and saw he had closed half the distance already.

I pushed the bicycle over and let out a shout of pure, terrified frustration. There was no one to hear. I was alone up against a tireless foe.

I left the bike and ran.

"Stop! I will not hurt you!" Bullethead bellowed.

"Yeah, right!"

Not too far down the path I entered a park with a lake. The sign read WESTCHESTER LAGOON. I pumped my arms as fast as I could as I raced on, but it was no use: Bullethead was reaching out for me again.

Suddenly, I had an inspiration for a plan that just might work. I drove my body forward. My training kicked in, and I did a roundoff back handspring into a double back tuck, landing at least eight feet out into the lake.

Splash!

The shock of the cold water took my breath away. It was deep, too; I couldn't touch the bottom. I blindly punched in front of me, but my pursuer wasn't there.

I lifted my gaze and saw Bullethead, standing in the grass,

arms folded across his chest.

"Get out of the water!" he ordered without a trace of breathlessness. "You must come with me!"

"Why don't you come in and get me? Oh, wait, did the boy genius forgot to make his toy robot waterproof? How sad! Looks like I'm out of reach. Oh well. Ha-ha."

He stared at me with a harsh expression while I continued to tease him like a five-year-old on the playground. I even took to splashing (I know, real mature).

I don't know why I was bothering to harass a machine. It didn't really make much sense. I guess I was feeling good about my small victory.

The good times wouldn't last, however.

"Miss Reynolds! You will not escape!"

He slipped off his coat and threw it to the ground. Then he yanked off his tie.

"What? No! You can't! You'll...rust or something!" I began paddling backward.

As he marched into the water, he ripped off his button-down shirt with a look of rigid determination.

The water did little to slow him down as he strode into the lake, not swimming, but walking, until all I could see was his head. And then that, too, disappeared below the surface.

Terror struck when I could no longer see him. I assumed he was still marching toward me along the sandy bottom.

I swam with all my might toward a tiny island in the center of the lake. When my arms got tired, I stopped for a moment, and swiveled in every direction, looking for him.

I felt something bump my foot. I screamed and swam hard

for another fifty yards.

Stopping again, I looked down for any sign of him. But the water was too dark. I couldn't see anything except my legs circling. I was hyperventilating, becoming dizzy with fear. It was like waiting to be attacked by a shark.

And just as I began to swim again, a hand reached up from the depths and grabbed my ankle.

Half a scream later, I was pulled under.

Bullethead dragged me along as he calmly walked toward the shore. I felt like a helium-filled float being pulled in a parade.

I wasn't sure if he knew that, as a human, I had to breathe. And we were a long way from shallow water. I would easily drown before we got there.

I kicked at his arm and his viselike grip, but it was no use.

In a last-ditch effort, I swam down to him using mostly my arms, and started punching and kicking at his steely body.

He let go of my ankle only to grab me, sling me over his hip like an unruly child, and continue his slow underwater march toward land.

If I didn't do something quick, I was going to drown. No reeducation necessary. My brain was screaming at my lungs to take a breath. Soon I would inhale, whether I wanted to or not, and water would painfully crash into my chest.

Good night, Gabby.

I wriggled and I twisted. I poked and I jabbed. I reached for hair that wasn't there. But it wasn't until I used my nails to scratch, and scratch hard, that I had any effect at all.

I gouged his artificial skin, and sparks began to pop and sizzle as water seeped into the bloodless wounds, flooding his electric circuitry. Strong shocks buzzed through my hands, zinged up my arms. His grip loosened, but I kept fighting, wielding my nails like an angry cat. I rotated my body and slashed at his face and arms.

Before long, we were engulfed in a whirlpool of electrical activity. Mini bundles of lightning darted from his forearms, nose, and cheeks. The water felt supercharged as he seemed to short-circuit completely. I finally had the upper hand.

Suddenly, he resembled a dozen bricks of firecrackers going off at the same time. His head started whipping uncontrollably from side to side while his arms flailed spastically at his sides.

He was past the point of no return. I swam toward the surface in triumph.

My last, murky image of Bullethead was of a twisted hunk of fiery metal lying on the bottom of the lake. He hardly resembled the creature that had given us *all* so much trouble over the past two days.

A deep breath had never felt as good as when I finally lifted my head out of the water and flung my hair out of my face.

But I didn't hang around. I swam for land until I was waist deep and then high-stepped it the rest of the way out of Westchester Lagoon.

I slogged my way back to the hotel, glancing over my shoulder every few steps, even though I knew I was no longer being pursued.

Bullethead was finished.

Chapter 14
The Big One

Easy... Careful...

The first thing I saw when I nudged open the door was my dad's legs, motionless on the bed. Otherwise, the hotel room looked empty. His door had been open a crack, while across the hall, mine was fully closed.

"Dad? It's me. Are you all right?" I asked in dread as I cautiously stepped into the room, heart pounding.

He looked lifeless lying there and offered no response. As I flew over to his side, I saw signs of a struggle all around the room. The end table lamp was knocked over, one of the chairs was flipped onto its side, and Dad's papers were strewn everywhere.

Kelvin, I will never forgive you for this.

I gave my dad a gentle shake but got no reaction. I put my head to his chest and heard a strong but slow heartbeat.

I breathed a sigh of relief that, at least, he was alive.

Tears flooded my eyes. I quickly wiped them away.

163

"Dad!" I shouted. "Dad! Wake up!"

I rocked him forcefully from side to side.

"Come on, wake up! Dad, what am I supposed to do?"

He grumbled a bit, turned onto his side, but would not be roused. Then I saw a trickle of dried blood and a tiny puncture wound on the side of his neck.

Oh no!

They had dosed my dad with that Sodium Pentothal stuff that they had given RJ!

I backed off in frustration and left him to his chemically induced slumber. Then it struck me: all the equipment was gone.

Kelvin had taken our evidence.

And, as Raven had pointed out, nothing was backed up.

"Oh, I'm gonna wring his scrawny little neck!"

I paced back and forth in the little hotel room as the reality of the situation hit me hard. I was stuck in Anchorage, Alaska, without any adult supervision, while the world was coming apart at the seams.

I decided it was time to call my mother and tell her everything. I needed help and I had nowhere else to turn.

Oh, she was going to be furious. But then she would calm down, like she always does, and figure a way to get me out of this mess.

Heck, she worked for the *mayor*. Perhaps she could send a fighter jet to come and pick me up or, at a minimum, one of those armored vehicles that the SFPD just bought from the military.

Feeling slightly hopeful, I raced into my room and quickly got changed out of my wet clothes. I grabbed my cell phone. It

164

was the only piece of modern technology that Kelvin had missed.

I turned it on, and to no great surprise, found I had no service. Well, I needed it for Mom's work number anyway, so I held on to it and went back over to my dad's room. I didn't want to leave him for too long.

Before calling, I flicked on the news so I could hear the adults talking and pretend that I wasn't quite so alone. I used the hotel's landline to call the San Francisco Mayor's Office.

I tried over and over again but got a busy signal every time.

At some point, the wind started howling, so I went over to the window for a peek outside. The sky was a mass of swirly black clouds with lightning strikes to the north—the direction of the Northern Lights facility.

Even though it would be harder to explain to the police than to my mother, I dialed 911.

No one answered.

I was shocked. *Are emergency services really too busy to help?* I wondered as the phone kept ringing and ringing. I was growing increasingly terrified. Who was left to help me?

I continued alternating calls between the police and my mother, feeling more and more desperate with every attempt. My fingers were shaking as I punched the buttons.

The news anchor jabbered on about how things had gotten worse throughout the day. The riots were spreading like a flu epidemic, and the natural disasters were intensifying.

Airplanes were grounded until further notice, and American highways were starting to resemble parking lots as too many people were trying to flee the major cities all at the same time.

The planet was on the brink of disaster. Kelvin was taking

his temper tantrum way too far. If he didn't turn off Big Bertha soon, he was going to destroy everything.

Then the telephone dropped out of my hands as I watched the most disturbing news piece of the day: two earthquakes, about an hour apart, had rocked central California. The first had struck near San Juan Bautista and the second was just north of Point Reyes.

Those two locations straddle San Francisco, I realized in horror. *Looks like Kelvin is just working on his aim.* If that was true, then it wouldn't be long before he hit the bull's-eye.

The little maniac was making good on his personal threat against me, to destroy my home city. And there was nothing I could do about it. And with all the energy waves he was shooting into the atmosphere, it was no wonder the phone service was all wacky.

I flicked off the TV. I simply couldn't take any more bad news.

My dad and RJ were mind-wiped zombies, and Kyle and Raven were on their way to Juneau, probably *driving* now that planes were grounded. My mom and the police were completely out of touch, and I was hopelessly stuck in a hotel room a couple thousand miles away from home.

"Congratulations, Kelvin, you win!" I shouted. I walked over in despair and flopped down in one of the chairs.

Right away, I noticed a piece of paper on the table with an address for the Anchorage FBI, written in my dad's handwriting. He must have jotted it down while I had gone to the lobby earlier. The building was on the corner of Fifth Avenue and A Street.

I counted backward from I Street. It was only eight blocks away!

Since the police seemed to have their hands full, going to the FBI seemed like my next move. It was a last resort, but I had already tried the cops.

Surely the FBI could stop Kelvin. Then I could get help for my dad.

I wrote a quick note and left it on the table. If my father happened to wake up, I wanted him to know that I was more or less okay and that I had gone for help.

Just as I was setting the note down, I heard a large crash come from outside the hotel. My first thought was a car accident, but when I pulled back the curtain, I was shocked by what I saw.

Across the street from the hotel was a jewelry store. Someone had driven a car right through the storefront and was robbing the place. Bystanders weren't doing a thing to stop the theft. In fact, many people were going inside and grabbing small fortunes for themselves. I saw two guys fighting over a sack full of stolen treasure.

Craziness.

I scanned up and down Fifth Avenue. Cars were zipping down the one-way street at dangerous speeds, streetlights were blinking yellow, crowds were gathering here and there on street corners, and police cars were zooming through intersections at top speeds in a meager attempt to keep order.

There was no question of it in my mind: the riots had come to Anchorage.

I pondered the eight blocks to the FBI office and started shaking. Tears rushed into my eyes again, and this time I couldn't hold them back.

I sat on the floor, dropped my head into my hands, and lost it.

Chapter 15
Anger Management

About twenty minutes later, I had gotten enough control over myself to head downstairs and attend to the small matter of saving the world. I couldn't just hide in my hotel room all day and simply wish the chaos away.

Kelvin's deathray had to be affecting me, too. For a person who was usually very much in control of her emotions, I was feeling everything from weepy to angry, and flip-flopping back and forth so fast it was making my head spin. It was hard to think clearly.

I pushed the hotel door open and stepped out into the exact circumstances my mother had tried so hard to shelter me from all summer: an out-of-control city where lawlessness and anarchy reigned.

The first thing I noticed was how oppressively dark it had become. Normally there would be hours and hours of daylight left, but the thick black clouds blocked out the sun completely, making the sky nearly pitch black. Even the streetlamps were fooled and had popped on early. Their light shimmered in the eerie energy of the night.

I flinched at the lightning that steadily cut the darkness with shocks of white, yellow, and red. It rained down on the city in blinding fits of rage, as though each bolt emanated from the tip of one of Kelvin's vengeful fingers. The thunder that followed vibrated glass windows all around the city.

The air was heavy and charged, like if you touched anything metallic, you'd get a thousand-volt shock. Even under my long sleeves, I could feel the hairs on my arms standing on end. The back of my neck felt as if it were being lightly tickled.

I flipped up my hood and stayed close to the buildings as I made my way up Fifth Avenue. I tried not to make eye contact with anyone I passed, especially the people talking or mumbling to themselves.

One guy yelled gibberish in my face and then kept on moving. His breath reeked of alcohol.

Cars quickly darted down the street, blinding me with their headlights. My eyes felt unusually sensitive to the brightness.

"Repent! Repent! The end is near!" A wild-eyed man was harassing people as they passed the cathedral across the street. "The sun shall turn to sackcloth, the moon to blood! Earthquakes, floods, natural disasters! All signs that we are close! Don't deny the truth all around you, my brothers and sisters! Run away from this evil darkness! Repent *now*, before it's too late!"

I hurried across H Street, leaving his apocalyptic ramblings behind. Still, the guy had a point. It was hard to deny that it looked like Armageddon everywhere I turned.

Seven more blocks to go.

Soon I passed a couple of mean-faced bouncers providing security outside of two neighboring restaurants. Peeking through the windows as I went, it appeared as if nothing had changed on the inside.

A hostess was seating a family of four, waiters and waitresses were scurrying through the aisles with massive plates of food, and everywhere I looked, glassy-eyed customers were stuffing their faces.

Sheeple!

Having grown somewhat accustomed to the new reality, it was an odd sight. The people in there were going about their lives as if everything were normal—fiddling while Rome burned. I just wanted to go inside and shake them until they woke up from their artificial, mind-numbed worlds. But I left them to their illusions and crossed over G Street.

Up ahead, I heard a series of loud smashes that froze me in my tracks. I eased my way into the shadows. The path forward didn't seem so safe, but the people crossing the street behind me looked even worse. The bouncers I had passed were too far away to give me any protection. I was woefully on my own.

I tightened my grip on the canister of bear repellent in my hoodie pocket. I had taken it with me from my dad's room, just in case. It made me feel only slightly less anxious. I flicked off the safety with my thumb and kept moving forward.

I found out what had made the smashing noises only a block later. Just past F Street there was a fully enclosed skyway that crossed over Fifth Avenue. Some jerks had tossed a couple of street signs right through the windows. A ONE WAY sign stuck halfway through the glass, dangling precariously over the sidewalk below. I had no choice but to slink underneath it, my feet crunching on broken glass.

More commotion to my right caught my attention as I watched a bunch of punks running across Town Square Park. They shouted off into the distance, obviously the ones responsible. But at least they were going away, leaving me alone to continue with my task.

I relaxed my shooting hand ever so slightly just as the ONE WAY sign crashed to the ground behind me. My body uncontrollably flinched and I accidently sprayed the capsaicin inside my sweatshirt. Even though it wasn't a direct hit, I could smell the strong peppery odor almost instantly.

"Oh great!" I shouted in frustration. "Of all the dumb luck! What am I? Some sort of a moron?" I was sounding remarkably similar to the crazies I had been seeing talking to themselves in all the nooks and crannies of Fifth Avenue.

Was I one of them now and just didn't know it?

I put the safety back on and tucked the canister into my jeans. I pulled the sweatshirt off over my head while holding my breath and chucked it into a nearby trash bin.

The pepper spray had got me pretty good. My eyes were stinging, my nose runny, and my breath wheezy. I used my shirt to wipe my face and hands as best I could and continued stumbling toward my destination, uncomfortable and feeling ever more confused.

The farther I went, the more the city was freaking me out. I wasn't sure how much more I could take before I snapped. It felt like, at any moment, I could be thrown into a full-blown panic attack...or worse.

And where are the police? Whatever happened to protect and serve?

Although I heard the occasional siren, there was a distinct lack of law enforcement. I figured they must have been too overwhelmed and simply went home to protect and serve their own families.

Through the shopping district, there was a constant stream of people pouring out of the mall and nearby stores with their arms full of stolen merchandise. I heard a few shop owners' feeble attempts to stem the flow of looters, but for the most part, it was a free-for-all.

Fortunately, they were so intent on what they were doing that nobody paid any attention to the coughing, pepper-scented girl mumbling to herself as she walked down the street. I had become just another actor in the show.

There was a growing part of me, however, that wanted to join in the mayhem. Kelvin had Big Bertha cranked up so high it was hard to resist the urge to be...well, bad. Despite my best efforts to talk myself down from the edge, I was feeling an overwhelming desire to give in. It would have been so easy to let go.

"Don't give in, Gabby," I muttered. "Remember what Kelvin said...willpower, willpower, willpower. I am strong. I can beat this. Willpower! I control my thoughts! I control my thoughts! Nobody out there is gonna control me! I know what's real and what's a mind game! I'm not one of the sheeple!"

My utterances helped enough to resist the temptation to steal stuff I didn't want or need and keep me moving forward.

Just past C Street, I heard a cacophony of car alarms going off somewhere up ahead. The noise grew in intensity until I was forced to cross the street and slip past the commotion on the other side. It seemed that every car at the local rental place had been awoken from a deep sleep at the same time.

I ran the rest of the way to A Street and finally arrived at the imposing Anchorage FBI building. I went to the front door, only to find it locked.

"Help me! Somebody, please! Is anybody in there?"

I knocked and banged and shouted, but nobody came to the door. Some FBI agent in there had to have heard the ruckus I was making!

I ran out of patience and went in search of another entrance. I passed a window with a bright light and stopped to get a better look. There were people inside.

Desks and chairs were pushed aside and they were standing in a circle. In the center were two men in a fistfight. The spectators were shouting and instigating the two warriors.

I stared in disbelief. Kelvin had gotten to the FBI, too!

After all that, risking my life, my mission had proved yet another colossal failure.

I started pounding on the window anyway, like a crazy person. "Help! We need you out here! Come on! Help us! Ahhh!"

I turned around to leave, only to come face to face with a soulless grin. "I'll help ya, cutie. You don't hafta pay me nuffin'."

The man looked like living rot as he aggressively stepped forward.

"Ahhh!" I whipped out the pepper spray and blasted him directly in the mouth before he could get to me.

He started to choke and gag—at that moment, and without warning, I went nuts. I could no longer fight it. I ran down the street screaming uncontrollably. Something in me had finally snapped and I was turned into a primitive, more barbaric version of Gabriella Reynolds. I only wanted to yell and tear and scratch and bite. I didn't want to fight the wicked rage any longer.

I wanted to let my fury loose.

My willpower fully dissolved into the overwhelming stench of a seething witch's cauldron that had just bubbled over.

But then, all of a sudden, loud cracks and pops rang out all across the city—only, they weren't gunshots, they were power plants and transformers and fuses blowing.

Like a tidal wave crashing over the city, a rolling blackout swept through Anchorage, instantly casting us back into the Stone Age.

In the blink of an eye, the electricity was gone. That was the last straw for me. I went full-out psycho, howling and hooting like a wild savage down Fifth Avenue.

Running blindly, barely aware of what I was doing, I was cut off by the loud screech of tires. A door painted with flames whooshed open. I cowered away from the overhead light.

"Gabby, is that you?" I heard a male voice.

"Whoa, what's wrong with her?"

Before I knew it, I was forcefully thrown into the back of a vehicle.

The door slammed shut and the vehicle sped away.

And even though the blue shag inside of the van seemed vaguely familiar, I kept screaming in terror.

Chapter 16
Gabbing Away

"Gabby! It's me, Kyle!"

"Stay away from me! You...you robot *freak*!" I screamed, kicking my legs wildly at the metal-headed creature.

I almost fell as the van whipped around a dark corner.

"Robot? It's just me and Raven! Look!" He flipped back his shiny makeshift hood so I could see his face. I *did* recognize him, but I was not in my right mind. "We're trying to help you!"

"You're t-tricking me. You...and her...y-you're more of K-Mack's *machines*!" I ran my fingers through my hair in frustration. "I'm confused. I can't think straight!"

"It's because your mind is all wacked out on EMFs, hon! If you would just trust me for a second and wrap this around your head, you'll be able to think more clearly." He held out a large slice of some shiny material. "It's an emergency thermal blanket, Gabby. Drape it over your head and shoulders like a babushka...you know, a scarf. You'll notice a difference right away."

I reluctantly did as he requested.

As soon as my head was covered, I got some instant relief. The buzzing sound disappeared and I began to feel a sense of ease spread throughout my body.

I sat down in the middle of the van, pulled the shiny material all the way across my face, dropped my head forward, and closed my eyes. After a few deep breaths, I was feeling considerably improved.

I can't believe it. The Tinfoil Hat people were right all along.

When I finally opened up a crack, Kyle was smiling at me.

"The Mylar's a pretty effective buffer, isn't it? Stay right there. I'm just going to attach this grounding wire to the bottom of the shield. Raven rigged it to the old CB radio. This will really help to draw the bad EMFs away from you." He reached out his hand. "You're not going to bite me, are you?"

"No, of course not." I held still while he took a small metal clip and attached it to the blanket.

"Feeling better?" he asked when I was sufficiently grounded.

I smiled weakly. "Yeah. Thanks."

Kyle flipped up his Mylar hood while Raven barreled on through the darkened streets of Anchorage. She, too, wore the shiny protective headgear.

A few turns later, Raven pulled the vehicle into a deserted parking lot somewhere on the edge of town. She parked the truck behind a small grove of trees. Then she cut the engine and killed the headlights. The only light came from a small overhead bulb and the frequent lightning strikes.

"I am so glad to see you guys. I thought...well, I thought I was a goner. I was trying so hard to fight the mind control. I just couldn't. It was too strong."

"Well, don't worry. Kelvin can't get to you under there. You're safe now," Kyle said.

"Thank you guys for saving me."

"Where's your dad?" Raven asked.

"Oh, Raven, they zapped him," I said, my voice shaky as I tried to fight back tears. "Just like RJ. Kelvin came to Anchorage with Dr. Hitzig and a gang of thugs and they mind-wiped him. He's passed out in the hotel room. I couldn't wake him up."

"We need to go get him, right now!" Kyle said.

"Honestly, I think we should leave him be. The building has security, and with Kelvin long gone, he's safer from the crazies in there than we are out here at the moment. But Raven...they stole all of your equipment, with all the evidence. I'm sorry. There was nothing I could do."

"I see," she said through gritted teeth, not making eye contact. She gently pulled on the dashboard wire that connected to my blanket as if she were checking the connection.

"How did *you* escape with your brain intact?" Kyle asked.

"I slipped away and ran. Had to destroy Kelvin's bodyguard...who, by the way, was a robot."

"What?" said Kyle.

"Hmm, that kind of makes sense," mumbled Raven.

"What are you guys doing here, anyway? I figured you'd be in Juneau by now."

Kyle sat down next to me.

"We dropped RJ off at his parents' house in Homer. And he was talking and actually making sense when we got there. The

178

effects of the mind wipe were wearing off, at least somewhat. He asked about you and your dad. And it's only about thirty hours since they tried to sauté the man's brain."

"The guy's a tank," said Raven. "He'll be fine."

"That's encouraging," I said, thinking of my dad.

"So, Mr. Hopper, RJ's pop, drove us over to the local airfield—I was just going to leave the van with him for a while—when we found out that nobody was allowed to take off, like, anywhere on the *planet*."

"Yeah, I heard that on the news," I said while Raven pulled the material further down on my forehead.

"Leave it right there," she said, and pointed in my face.

I did as she ordered. I didn't care that I looked like a total dork.

"It's a long drive to Juneau," Kyle continued, "and since the route takes us right through Anchorage, we decided to stop and see how you guys were making out. If you needed any help."

"It was just dumb luck that we saw you bolting down Fifth Avenue," Raven added. "What the heck were you doing out there, anyway?"

I explained my futile attempt to tell the FBI about Kelvin. "But they were no help," I concluded. "And if we don't tell the authorities what's really causing this—or rather, who—Kelvin is just going to keep cranking up his deathray."

"You've got a good point there," Kyle said.

"So who do we tell?" I asked. "I mean, the cops are either running all over the city trying to control the chaos or have just given up. The FBI wouldn't come to the door. But, more importantly, *how* would we tell them? Cell towers are down.

Landlines are shot."

"We have to do *something*!" Kyle said.

"And soon," Raven agreed. "Within a few more hours the world is going to be back to horse-and-carriage days." She raised a fist to the ceiling. "Thank you very much, Kelvin, you little *monster*!"

As if the nerd himself answered her declaration, lightning flashed directly overhead and lit up the inside of the van with a million watts of power. The thunder that followed was deafening.

I pulled the Mylar blanket tightly around my face until it settled down. Of course, if we got hit by lightning wearing metal hats...geez.

"Hey!" I shouted a few moments later. "I think I might have an idea!"

"What?" they said in unison.

"Is there any way we could use the van's CB radio to get in touch with the government? I mean, like the real government— the top people in Washington who give the orders. I bet they're tuned in all up and down the radio with everything that's going on. I'm sure *someone* in DC would like to hear what we have to say."

"CBs are only short range, Gabby," said Raven. "On the other hand... Hmm. I guess I could tweak it to go hundreds or even thousands of miles."

"Yeah?" I asked, perking up.

"There's just one problem. Even if by some miracle they do believe us, practically *half* of the whole radio wave spectrum is reserved for the government. Trying to tune in to the right frequency would be like trying to find a needle in a haystack—in ten-thousand haystacks. Lastly, *it's illegal.* I could go to jail for broadcasting on government frequencies."

"I don't see any other options here," Kyle said soberly.

"There isn't going to be any jail, or government, or anything, if we don't stop this," I said. "What do we have to lose?"

Raven crinkled up her face as she considered what to do.

"Okay, I'll do it. But Kyle, I need you to drive me to higher ground—the higher the better—while I mess with the resonator, make some adjustments to the capacitor..."

Raven grabbed her tool bag and got right to work, babbling, mostly to herself, about the technical aspects of turning a CB radio into a long-range communicator.

"I know just the place," Kyle said with a certain twinkle in his eye. "Sultana Drive. Took a few girlfriends up there back in the day."

"Ew!" I scoffed. "Too much information, dude."

Kyle laughed and made his way to the front of the van, flopping down in the driver's seat. "Hang on!" he said as he fired up the engine and took off like a maniac, driving wildly through the chaotic streets of Anchorage.

I nervously clutched the sides of my seat. There was a part of me that wished I were just one of the unknowing, terrified masses, hunkering down in their homes waiting for it all to blow over. But in my heart I knew that Kelvin would keep punishing his fellow man, and me, until he'd had his fill of revenge.

About twenty-five minutes later, we entered a park at the top of a huge hill at the end of a windy road. Kyle pulled the van into a spot and cut the engine.

No one else was there.

I jumped out to have a look around while Raven finished up her techie work.

Although she had unhooked the grounding wire, I was not about to part with my thermal blanket. In fact, I tied it into a very cool knot at the base of my skull and pulled out several locks of hair to frame my face. I was sure it would eventually be all the rage in post-apocalyptic fashion.

But until the nightmare was over, I had no intention of taking it off. I never wanted to experience such confusion and anger again.

In the distance, the city of Anchorage was still being pelted by jagged bolts of lightning. Cook Inlet looked inky black.

Cars darted here and there, but we were too far away for me to make out any people. Maybe if I had binoculars.

I saw a couple of emergency vehicles flashing red and white lights, so at least some of the public services were still in operation.

But for how long?

"It's ready!" Raven called to me. "Let's get started! This is going to take a *long* time!"

I walked over to the open side door. Raven shoved the handset into my face.

"Me?" I shouted.

"Hey, you're the one named Gabby. You don't expect me to do the talking? I'd end up biting somebody's head off. Besides, I need to adjust the frequencies. We have about"—she did a quick calculation in her head—"150 million kilohertz of bandwidth to slowly scroll through. And Yack, he's going to be assisting me."

Kyle offered some words of encouragement. "You can do this, Gabby. Be commanding, authoritative, and persuasive. Try to channel some of that Chase Reynolds personality. Make your father proud."

"Just press your fingers on the button and start talking," Raven instructed. "Every couple of sentences, pause and let go, so we can see if we've caught any big fish. You won't hear anyone responding while you're pressing that button down and talking, okay? And don't worry about what we're doing over here. You just talk and talk and talk until somebody out there gets the message. We'll do the rest."

"Okay," I said, feeling a bit quivery, as if the stage lights had suddenly been turned on for the most important performance of my life.

I was attached to the radio by a twisted cord, so I couldn't go very far. Not very good for someone so hyperactive. I held my fingers over the button, but suddenly couldn't think of anything to say.

I paced three steps in each direction, waiting for inspiration to strike.

"Just start off by telling 'em what you know," said Kyle. "Most of the time there won't be anyone there to hear you anyway, so don't be nervous. It's just for that one time someone is listening, you need to be convincing and making sense."

I took a deep breath and finally pressed the button. "Um, hello. This is Gabby Reynolds. I'm coming to you from Anchorage, Alaska. I'm from California, going into the seventh grade. I hope we don't get in trouble for using these frequencies, but this is an emergency. I have important information for anyone high up in the United States government. Repeat, this is an emergency. Is there anyone out there?"

I let go of the button.

Nothing but an empty *hisss* came from the speakers.

"You gotta keep going," Raven urged. "149,999,999 kilohertz to go."

"Sheesh."

"You're doing great," she said.

I pressed the button again. "The Northern Lights facility, just outside of Fairbanks, Alaska, has been hijacked. The antenna field is being used as a weapon by a Dr. Kelvin Mackowsky. I know this is going to sound strange, well, maybe not to the right person, but he and his followers are totally responsible for all the chaos that's happening around the world. All of it! The power outages. The earthquakes. The floods. The riots. He's using mind control to make people angry and violent. And that machine, Big Bertha, can apparently control the weather, too. Freaky stuff, I know. Someone needs to do something. The government. I don't know? Send in the Marines. This is not a prank! Please, does anyone read me?"

Hisss.

I looked over at my two partners in crime and gave them a shrug.

"You can talk about things that someone would only know from being inside the facility and meeting with Kelvin," Kyle suggested.

"Good idea." I squeezed the button. "Here are a few accounts to prove that I'm not some conspiracy theory freak." I paused for a moment, realizing I was standing there with my

184

head wrapped up in Mylar, looking quite the part of a nutcase.

I shook it off and continued.

"I want to verify that I've actually been inside the facility and have met with Dr. Mackowsky. First off, Dr. Kelvin Mackowsky likes to go by the nickname K-Mack. He's a thirteen-year-old brat who wears thick glasses and black clothes—including a ridiculous turtleneck. Yuck! He has a really short temper, too. My goodness, you have to be careful what you say to him. For a supervillain, he's kind of a total drama king. Hypersensitive much? Also, he's a complete cheeseball with girls. And his breath smells like tuna."

Kyle laughed at that one.

Hisss.

Still nothing.

What else, what else...

"He builds robots in his spare time. He has an RFID chip implanted into his ankle so his CIA handlers know where he is at all times. Oh! He has taken them hostage, by the way! One of them is this tall blond lady. I tried to rescue her, but I couldn't. There are others...good people that are being used for experiments."

Hisss.

"Um, the facility has an observation room on the fifth floor. The prisoners are being held in the living quarters on the seventh floor. And the nerve center for the entire building is on the top floor—Kelvin's control room."

Hisss.

That was the basic communication.

I talked to nobody for over seven hours straight. I had

repeated variations of the same message at least a thousand times. I was physically exhausted, my throat hurt, and my voice was sounding more and more like RJ's, but I just kept on talking.

Every once in a while, somebody would respond, but it always turned out to be a dead end. Just some prepper messing with a ham radio, wondering if it was time to break out the bottled water and stored beans.

I had been awake for nearly two days straight. And in that time, I had seen things that no twelve-year-old should ever have to witness. I had endured a bizarre visit with K-Mack, escaped from a high-security government facility, defeated Bullethead the cyborg, and survived, against all odds, on the mean streets of Anchorage, Alaska.

It was all starting to catch up to me, but I jabbered on.

As I did, I thought about the Northern Lights facility and all the wickedness Big Bertha was inflicting on every living creature. What it had done to those whales...

Why build such a device in the first place? I wondered. *It's only a matter of time until things like that fall into the wrong hands.*

I felt sad and responsible for all of the people that Kelvin had hurt or put in harm's way since we'd snooped through his lab. Life's waters were tricky enough to navigate without some boy genius freak throwing a cyclone in your path.

And after so many hours of talking, I didn't think I was even making sense anymore. Everything that came out of my mouth was sounding like random gobbledygook.

"...Yeah, so right, it's me, Gabby Reynolds, again. I'm still here. Your delirious host for tonight's broadcast. So, let me repeat, for like the *billionth* time, that it's all Dr. Mackowsky's fault. I mean K-Mack's fault. Oh, who cares what he wants to be called? He's nothing but a spoiled baby having a major temper tantrum. He's up there messing with things that shouldn't be messed with. The ionosphere! Really? Who messes with the ionosphere? *Hello!* We earthlings kind of *need* the ionosphere. What if they break it? That's gonna be some *real* global warming for you there, folks."

Hisss.

"Hmm, how would I describe K-Mack? He's extremely clever but diabolical at the same time. He wants more than anything to be free, which I can understand after my own mother kept *me* a prisoner for weeks. Well, Kelvin's been a prisoner his whole life; it's no wonder he snapped. I'm not saying his actions are acceptable, obviously, but come on.

"So he's decided to take it all out on us. Yes, *sorry*, folks, you're the victim of someone else's poor parenting. That's right, ladies and gentleman, there it is, I said it. Bad parenting affects us all. Kids need to, well, just be kids for a while. They need to run, and play, and ride their bikes, and go to parties. Yes, of course, they need rules and curfews and boundaries, but they don't need to be put to work designing weapon systems for DARPA while they're still in diapers!"

Oh, I'm so off track.

Kyle and Raven wouldn't even look at me, I was being such a weirdo.

In truth, what I really wanted to do was smash the stupid handset on the ground and call it a night. And that wasn't the mind control talking. That was pure frustration.

I'd had it.

"Does anyone out there *care*?" I shouted into the handset at my wit's end. "Ugh! Can anyone on this entire planet even stinkin' hear me?!"

Hisss.

"I can't take it anymore!" I yelled up to the sky as I tossed the handset into the back of the van. "That's enough!"

The sound of my outburst echoed off the mountains. I dropped my head in defeat.

"Yeah, we read you loud and clear, Miss Reynolds. Copy that," a crackly male voice said over the CB.

What? I quickly grabbed the handset and pressed the button.

"Who's there? Come in! Who is this?"

"I'm a system administrator with the National Security Agency, code name Opal Equinox."

I glanced at Kyle and Raven in disbelief. The two looked shocked, but they froze in place. They clearly didn't want to accidentally lose the signal.

"You know you're on restricted airwaves?" he said, without a hint of humor in his voice.

"Are we in trouble?"

"Under the circumstances, I think we can agree to look the other way."

"Thank you, sir. So, are you going to stop him?"

"Yes, we are sending in a Special Forces team as we speak to neutralize the situation and extract the prisoners. Well done! Your president, your country, and all of us here at the NSA, thank you for your service, ma'am, and umm"—he lowered his voice—"your parenting advice."

"Huh?"

"That's all for now. Over—"

"Oh, he is *so* grounded!" a female voice jumped in before the transmission cut out. "This is the most embarrassing—"

Click.

We stared at each other, dazed, for a moment.

When it finally sank in that they had patched us through to Dr. and Dr. Mackowsky, Kelvin's parents, all three of us exploded with laughter.

I did, however, feel a little weird about bad-mouthing their son in front of the world.

Kyle got out of the van and gave me a double high five.

Raven grabbed me by the shoulders. "Nicely done. Way to hang in there. I knew you could do it." She then showed a glimpse of her human side by giving me a big hug.

I giggled over her shoulder at the unusual display of affection.

Kyle and Raven walked over to the edge of the parking lot for a well-deserved stretch and a moment to stare out at the view.

It was one of those rare occasions of victory that I would savor for a long time.

Feeling stiff, I stretched a little myself, but I was mostly just tired and hoarse.

Although the lightning continued to brighten up the sky to the west, I decided to take full advantage of the darkness, and climbed into the back of the van for some rest.

Dad would be proud of me, I thought, as I snuggled down into the shaggy blue carpet. The van really was kind of cool. It had grown on me.

Figuratively, not literally.

The madness wasn't over yet, and there would be tons of cleanup to be done, but my role was complete. I felt an overwhelming sense of calm that I had done everything in my power to help, and just wanted to crash until it was all finished.

Let someone else save the world for a change.

Chapter 17
K-Mack's Last Stand

Confidence, power, intimidation...

In the control room of Northern Lights, Kelvin heard the unmistakable *whoosh-whoosh* of helicopter blades several miles out. He knew immediately they weren't the typical single-engine choppers often found in central Alaska, but were government issued.

Growing up around military bases had trained his ears well. *Besides*, he thought, *who else but Army grunts would be flying on such a nasty night?*

"Aim Big Bertha straight up, Dr. Figgs! Trajectory, infinity! Hurry!" he yelled.

"But that would mean—"

"I know what it means, you imbecile!" Kelvin rudely cut him off. "I'm in control of this operation to the end! Now do it!"

"Yes, Dr. K-Mack."

Dr. Figgs went to work tweaking dials, pressing buttons, and flipping switches.

The ground rumbled as Big Bertha slowly moved into position.

The world's youngest supervillain had known that there was always a chance he might have to put his final contingency plan into action. Nevertheless, he was surprised they had figured him out. The loss of his K-bot was a huge blow to the operation, but he was sure that he had still covered all of his bases.

It had to be that gazelle girl. He felt it in his bones and in the constant throbbing of his left temple where she had kicked him. *She's a crafty one, all right.*

Kelvin glanced out the window just in time to see black-clad soldiers rappelling to the ground from open helicopter doors. An intimidating sight, to be sure.

The raid was on.

"Cool outfits," he mumbled as he turned his attention back to the control panel. "I'm going to need an initial oscillator of ten to the negative three kilohertz. I'll take care of the pulsed SHF follow-up. You just hold her steady. No wave vacillations. No matter what."

"Of course."

As Kelvin waited for the antenna field to cycle up, he walked over to the security monitors and watched the Special Ops troops storm the front door. Once through, they raced down the first-floor corridor, guns drawn.

"On the ground! On the ground! Hands where we can see 'em!"

Kelvin watched as several of his subordinates, including Dr. Ambry, surrendered. "Come on," he grumbled, peering over at the main phase indicator dial. He was tapping his foot, a sure sign that his confidence was faltering.

Into the stairwells they poured.

Kelvin watched anxiously as the Special Forces soldiers captured each floor they entered. The well-trained men were methodically taking the facility one level at a time. Aside from the thuggish orderlies, who had to be forcefully subdued, there was very little resistance.

Almost there...

Most of the lower-floor monitors had gone out. It was standard operating procedure when seizing an enemy compound to remove the commander's eyes and ears. They were sticking to protocol.

Kelvin watched in astonishment as all of the Residential G-Block doors popped open simultaneously. Someone must have flipped the master switch.

Slowly the captives emerged from their cells, realizing, one by one, that they were free from their cages.

They looked like the walking dead, as if they had been buried alive and, newly arising from the ground, were seeing bright light and breathing the fresh air for the first time in years.

Kelvin snickered when he realized that the notion wasn't too far from the truth. He quickly stopped giggling, however, when he saw what happened next.

"Don't touch me!" an all-too-familiar voice boomed through one of the seventh-floor speakers.

Kelvin scanned three monitors down to see the action.

"I vill come wiz you peazfully, *ja*. Zhere is no need to be rough, *mein guter Mann*."

K-Mack watched as Dr. Hitzig only pretended to be obedient

and then, suddenly, made a last-ditch attempt to escape. He lunged forward and jabbed the apprehending soldier in the neck with a fully loaded syringe. He hit the plunger and ran out into the hallway, leaving the drugged warrior slowly collapsing to the floor.

More black-clad soldiers out in the hall yelled at the fleeing physician, trying to detain him. But Dr. Hitzig ran the other way, through a pair of double doors, and down a long hallway.

Right into the center of G-Block.

Kelvin cringed but couldn't take his eyes off the horrifying, yet strangely riveting, scene.

Dr. Hitzig skidded to an abrupt halt. Dread spread across his features as he turned a slow circle and appeared to fully grasp the danger he now faced. He was hemmed in on all sides by a mob of angry patients.

His patients! His *laborratten*, or lab rats, as he was so fond of calling them.

They closed in on him with vengeance in their eyes and wicked grins on their lips. Dr. Hitzig looked terrified. He didn't even attempt to defend himself.

One of Kelvin's CIA handlers, John Barnes, took the first swing and clocked him in the nose, hard. Bright red fluid gushed from his nostrils, but he didn't fall. Kelvin's other handler, Samantha Wilkes, took the next shot by leaping into the air and kicking him in the chin.

He fell straight back, landing with a *thud*.

Kelvin watched in morbid fascination as the newly freed victims took turns pummeling the doctor—when suddenly, that monitor went out, too.

The seventh floor was taken.

Well, they'll never get me.

"How we doing, Dr. Figgs?"

"Um, looks like we're about a minute away, sir."

One by one, Kelvin watched as the bank of monitors went out, until only one image remained: the long view down the thirteenth-floor hallway.

Kelvin swung his head back and forth between that image and the indicator dial, which, at that point, seemed to be creeping up toward its mark at a snail's pace.

"Here they come!" Kelvin shouted.

Kelvin had to admit: those guys were good. He was super impressed. In just a few short minutes, they had captured the entire building.

Wow, they really sent the dang SEAL Team Six or whatever for little ole me? How flattering.

Under different circumstances he might have very much enjoyed watching their takeover, but considering *he* was their main target, his heart was pounding and, this time, he was the one sweating like a pig.

"On my mark, Dr. Figgs. In five...four..."

The last of the security cameras was destroyed.

"Three...two..."

The door was busted down and into the room swarmed the Special Forces soldiers.

"One..."

The last thing Kelvin remembered seeing was the puzzled look on the commander's face when the old man and the dorky boy standing in front of him slipped on shiny tinfoil hats.

"Now!"

Within seconds, everyone fell to the ground.

Well...almost everyone.

# # #

A little while later, I was sitting with Kyle and Raven on the back bumper of the van watching the sunrise.

The sky was a swath of red, yellow, and blue shot through with golden rays that most certainly pointed the way to heaven. The lightning had stopped earlier, and the clouds had gradually cleared. The air no longer felt charged, and there was an overwhelming sense of calm. Even without our protective headgear.

We wanted to wait for daybreak before heading back into the city.

A sudden buzzing in my pocket startled me, until I realized what it was. "Hey! Somebody's calling me! The towers are back!" I yanked out the phone. "It's my mother, guys. Shhh, don't talk. Hi, Mom!"

"Gabby! Are you all right?"

"Yeah, I'm fine, Mom. Are you?"

"Oh, thank goodness. We're good here, just a lot of shaking. I've been worried about you! You're not going to believe what is happening a few hundred miles north of Anchorage!"

"Oh, you might be surprised. Try me."

I put my mother on speakerphone so Kyle and Raven could hear as well. They remained quiet the whole time.

With all that was going on in the city and the mayor's office, she didn't have long to talk, but was able to give a brief rundown of what her inside sources were telling her.

She informed us about the Special Forces predawn raid on the Northern Lights facility, the capture of the rogue scientists, and the release of several prisoners.

Everything she said was not hard to believe at all, until right at the end.

"Everyone at the facility just mysteriously collapsed," she said. "They were okay about an hour later, perhaps a little groggy, but they all just passed out. At the exact same time, Gabby! And the rumor is that the ringleader, a Dr. Kelvin Mackowsky, may have escaped. All they found was a bloody RFID chip that they think he cut out of his own leg."

Our jaws dropped in disbelief. *He got away?*

"Well, at least it seems to be over now," Mom continued. "The riots have all fizzled out, the tremors have stopped, and the weather is better. I really gotta go, sweetheart. Hey, how's your father?"

"Oh, he's okay. Just in his room...sleeping like a log." I shrugged at Kyle and Raven.

"Well, okay. See you soon. Love ya."

"I love you, too, Mom."

I hung up and looked at the others, still in shock. "Can you believe it? They didn't find him."

"Don't worry, he'll get what he's got coming to him," Raven said darkly.

"Yeah," Kyle chimed in. "After what he put everybody through? They better catch him! If he's doing this at thirteen, what'll he try when he's thirty?"

I didn't even want to think about that. Of course, knowing K-Mack, he'd probably end up a billionaire or something.

And me, maybe one day I'd become a wild radio philosopher. A place like Alaska makes you want to try to tackle big things...

We sat there until all of the beautiful colors in the sky dissolved into a bright blue and the sun warmed our faces.

"Shall we get a move on?" I asked.

"We better go check on your dad," Kyle said.

"Yeah, he might need his diaper changed," Raven joked.

"Whoa, you mean there's a sense of humor lurking behind that hard exterior?" I teased.

"Harrumph," was all she said, and climbed into the van.

We drove down the hill in silence.

Once in the city proper, all around us were damaged buildings, broken-down vehicles, and garbage strewn all over the sidewalks. But there were already people pushing brooms and banging hammers. The big cleanup had begun. The hardworking people of Alaska weren't going to let a little chaos get them down.

As we pulled into the hotel's parking garage, my phone buzzed once again. This time it was a text. I was desperate to hear from one of my girlfriends back home, but when I tapped the screen...

No way.

Greetings, Gabby the Gazelle. It's your favorite punching bag. Don't worry, I forgive you. I'm off to the tropics for a while. Maybe I'll find a deserted island somewhere.

Goodbye, glaciers! Hello, sun, surf, and sand! But I'll be back, someday. Hey, maybe when I do we can go on that date. Dinner and a movie, huh, what a rip. I'll give you a buzz. K-Master. Ha, I changed my nickname.

So the little gnat *did* escape!

I read the text three times, not sure how to feel. The thought of him outraged me, and yet you had to respect a guy who was so determined to be free that he would cut an RFID chip from his own leg.

I bet his parents never saw that one coming.

But how did he get away? The facility was in the middle of nowhere.

No sooner had I asked the question than I got my answer in the form of another message. This time Kelvin had sent a picture of himself. He was wearing an Army baseball cap, dark Aviator sunglasses, big green earmuffs, and a goofy grin. One hand was firmly gripping a black control stick, while the other was giving the camera a super nerdy thumbs-up.

I could see blue sky and snowcapped mountains in the background. I had no idea who was taking the picture, but it didn't appear to be a selfie.

The caption read: *By the way, do you find helicopter pilots attractive?*

I had to laugh as I closed the message.

"What's so funny?" Kyle asked, pulling into a parking spot.

"Oh, nothing," I said with a grin as we got out of the van to go get my dad.

Strange how after all the trouble he'd caused, I couldn't

quite bring myself to hate the dork.

Maybe there was hope for the world yet.

Authors' Note

Dear Reader,

Not long ago, I was listening to talk radio on my way home from work when they began discussing the topic of *conspiracy theories.* If you don't know what that is, it's when someone believes that the public is being lied to. That people in power—the government, the media, celebrities, or anyone else that has the ear of the masses—is intentionally deceiving everybody for nefarious reasons.

I was surprised to learn that at least half of all Americans believe in one or more conspiracy theories. *Half!* Anything from little intrigues, like Elvis Presley faking his own death and living it up in South Florida, to humungous fabrications, like how the moon landings never actually happened and instead were produced in a Hollywood studio! Oh...and then there are the various storylines about who killed JFK or the idea that all the governments of the world really answer to a powerful group of shadowy elites who pull all the strings. The list is endless.

By the time I got home, I was determined to write a book that had something to do with conspiracy theories. My partner in crime loved the idea, and we got right to work planning and plotting. *Muahaha.*

So, after tons of research on conspiracy theories, *The Dork and the Deathray (50 States of Fear: Alaska)* was born.

And guess what? It's based on an actual conspiracy theory with scientists, antennas, and EMFs.

There is a real government facility in the wilderness region of Gakona, Alaska, called HAARP. They *claim* to be studying the ionosphere and advanced communication systems, but conspiracy theories about the place abound. Some people think the real-life antenna array can actually be used to generate floods, hurricanes, and even earthquakes. And others really do claim that adjusting the frequencies *can* allow scientists to use brain entrainment (see Chapter 5 – Bad Dreams) to bring people's mental states into harmony with a chosen frequency. In other words, *mind control*!

Have you heard of any bizarre conspiracy theories? If so, please write to us and tell us all about it. I'm not saying that we'll believe it, but I'm not *not* saying it, either.

In the meanwhile, many mysteries still await us across the fruited plain, so we hope you'll come along as our journey across America continues! If you're in the mood for a spine-tingling Southern ghost story, dare step into *The Haunted Plantation (50 States of Fear: Alabama)*. If werewolves are more your thing, try *Leader of the Pack (50 States of Fear: Colorado)*. And if you still can't get enough of paranormal creatures, we'd like to introduce you to a bigfoot of our acquaintance. Turn the page for a Bonus Chapter from *Bringing Home Bigfoot (50 States of Fear: Arkansas)*. Enjoy!

Thanks for reading,
E.G. Foley
(Eric & Gael)

Bringing Home Bigfoot

***"The Natural State" – Outdoorsman's Paradise...
with "Wild Man" sightings since 1846!***

The lone computer geek in a family of Eagle Scouts and football heroes, Nate Dunning would rather play video games than go camping any day. But after a run-in with the bully of the middle school, Nate's rugged, outdoorsman dad drags him out into Nature to toughen him up and teach him some survival skills. Just his luck, everything goes horribly awry when his dad forces him to stay out overnight in a tent all alone. Except that he isn't alone. Turns out the crazy old man at the country store was telling the truth. *"Thar's bigfoots in them woods!"* Talk about a hairy situation.

Chapter 1
Man Training

Gusting winds effortlessly tossed the mighty oaks back and forth. Dappled shadows danced in the dismal fall sunlight. The rustling leaves drowned out most other sounds.

Most other sounds, but not all.

"Hello!" I shouted at the dense forest as I stopped walking.

No response.

I jumped when a small creature scurried through the leaves. I quickly scanned every which way, but saw nothing threatening.

Probably just my imagination, I thought as I shook my head. But then...*snap,* I heard it again.

I whipped around. "Is someone there?" My voice cracked at the end. *Darn puberty!*

Eh, who was I kidding—I was no tough guy. Quite the opposite, actually. I was a wimp of the highest order. And for the past twenty minutes, I'd been hearing odd noises and having the strangest feeling that I was being followed.

But by whom? Or by...what?

I better keep moving.

I flipped my hood up to block out the scary sounds and continued along the windy path. (Hey, it works for the ostrich.)

It wasn't easy, however, to ignore my own voice mentally yelling at me to hurry up and get out of there.

It was a little over a three-mile hike from our family's cabin to the River Bend General Store. The path, for the most part, was clear, although, at times, I did have to climb over a few icky moss-covered logs, tiptoe around some sloppy mud puddles, and scurry through the underbrush when the trail seemed to disappear.

The underbrush was the worst. A home for all manner of ticks, spiders, snakes, rodents, and poisonous leaves. It was like wading through waist-high, shark-infested waters and not being able to see your feet. It was unnerving.

Another twenty minutes and I'd had enough. I still felt like I was being stalked, even with my head buried in the sand. I picked up my pace to a brisk walk, only to trip over an exposed root and fall onto my outstretched hands. It hurt my wrists.

"Did you get a good laugh at that?" I shouted to whoever or whatever was following me.

A thunderclap rumbled from somewhere in the distance as if chuckling at my clumsy display.

I stood up, brushed myself off, and kept trudging along.

I hated being so far from civilization. All this nature crud was totally not my speed. If I were to scream like a five-year-old girl at the top of my lungs, no would-be rescuer would hear me. I was utterly on my own against whatever might come my way.

Ignoring my own paranoia, I trudged up a long hill. My

arms were pumping, my thighs burning. (Hills are tough when you're out of shape.) Once at the top, I broke free from the clutches of the woods and entered a grassy park area that the locals call Lookout Point. Many different trailheads led to the place.

I flipped off my hood, looked up at the sky, and let out a big sigh of relief.

There were a couple of splintery old picnic tables and a rusted-out grill in the clearing. Empty bags of chips and spent bottles of pop littered the ground.

What is wrong with people? I picked up the trash and threw it in a nearby can. *What slobs! There, was that so hard?*

It wasn't far from the little park area to the store, but I sat down on one of the picnic tables to rest for a moment before pressing on. I slipped my backpack off my shoulders, took out a water bottle, and had a drink. My body seemed to relax considerably in the open, much-less-claustrophobic space.

From where I sat, I could see woods stretching for miles in all directions. The forest blazed with red, yellow, and orange leaves. Late October is always the best time of year to see the changing foliage.

Okay, fine, I admit it. Pretty spectacular.

I grabbed my binoculars to take a closer look. I scanned back and forth, admiring the once-a-year show. Way off to the west I spied the Buffalo River slicing a path through the trees like a giant serpent. Our cabin wasn't too far from that part of the river.

It was easy to see where the thunder had originated. A big storm was slowly rolling east across Northwest Arkansas.

Menacing clouds were heading my way. I had an ominous feeling that, in addition to whatever was pursuing me on foot, the storm was after me, as well.

It was as if all of the forces of nature were plotting against me, building, waiting, getting ready to pounce. *But why?* I didn't know, and it was freaking me out.

I reached into my pocket and grabbed an atomic-blast-flavored breath mint. No matter how many I ate, I couldn't "blast" the taste of squirrel out of my mouth. I wondered what my dad might force me to eat next. Leaves? Bugs? Dirt?

Earlier in the day, on his orders and against my better judgment, I had trapped a squirrel using nothing but wire, cord, and a few twigs. My dad taught me how to make a spring snare to trap small game. It was surprisingly easy, even for a nerd like me.

I had set several of them around the cabin, baiting the area with peanut butter. Mostly to appease my dad. I didn't think it was actually going to work. Squirrels must be *really* dumb.

Poor little thing was bouncing around like a fish caught on a line, freshly yanked out of the water. I felt bad for it. I had never trapped anything in my life. I couldn't watch as Dad "dispatched" the squirrel. That's just a big fancy hunting term for "hit it on the head until it was dead." I could never, ever do that. It was gross. Like, *splat*.

We cooked it over an open fire. Then Dad pulled it apart with his bare hands, acting like a caveman. He hadn't shaved in a while, so he sort of resembled one. Clearly, he was in his element when he handed me a dislocated leg with a proud smile on his rugged face and said, "Here ya go, son."

I think he thought that I would tear into it like a lion cub that hasn't eaten in weeks and thank him profusely for providing me with such great bounty. Instead, I held it like it was a dirty diaper and practically whined, "Ewww, is that hair? What is that brown stuff?"

"Just eat it, Nate," was his annoyed response. "It tastes like chicken. In the wild, you eat whatever protein source is available. You can't be finicky in a dynamic survival situation."

Well, we weren't in a "dynamic survival situation," but I pinched my nose and ate it anyway for fear that the Great Outdoorsman might disown me.

It didn't taste at all like chicken. It was stringy and tough. I wanted to gag, but I forced myself to swallow. The only good thing about eating squirrel is that there isn't very much of it. In a few bites, it was gone.

A loud rumble of thunder pulled me out of my thoughts. I packed up my gear and made my way to the other side of the park. Ducking under a low branch, I reentered the woods. I didn't want to get caught in a downpour.

I walked down the backside of the hill along a wider, much more frequented path. I was almost there.

Civilization! Or at least an outpost of it.

Even though I was being slowly tormented by some woodland creature—real or imagined—and despite the growing mass of foreboding clouds, it was nice to get a break from my dad. The guy's tough and is always riding me about something.

The two of us had been butting heads at the cabin almost nonstop for four days, ever since I was suspended from school. There was only so much "man training" I could take.

And let's face it, my dad thinks I'm a wimp. The worst part is, he's right. This camping trip was his best attempt to turn me from a ninety-pound eighth-grade lazybones into a menacing powerhouse. From a dorky weakling into a cast-iron mountain man.

Good luck with that, Dad.

Somehow I was born into a family of outdoor adventurers and jocks, subscribers to magazines like *Fishing World* and *Hunting Adventures* and *Crush the Competition*. A family made up of Bambi killers and overly muscled blockheads.

My parents have five sons and no daughters. Each one has more athletic ability than the next.

And then there's me, the youngest. I'm a gamer/computer geek with about as much coordination as a five-year-old learning to ride a bicycle. I hate sports and despise the great outdoors. I don't see the appeal.

More thunder boomed when I reached the bottom of the hill and stepped out of the forest for the second time. I quickened my pace as I made my way down the barren country lane that led to the nubby little shack of a store.

There were very few places to buy anything in the area, so the store carried everything from groceries to engine oil to camping supplies. I was heading there to buy some junk food, like any normal thirteen-year-old, but I was also going to satisfy another preoccupation of mine.

I was hopelessly addicted to video games and hadn't played at all in the four days since I'd gotten in trouble. I was experiencing some serious withdrawals. My thumbs were getting twitchy like they didn't know what to do with themselves.

Why else would I be walking alone through the woods, risking being mauled by an angry troop of squirrels avenging their fallen comrade?

The store had some old-school arcade games from the eighties like *Frogger*, *Pac-Man*, *Kung-Fu Master*, and *Donkey Kong* in the back. In the past, I never would have given such antiques a second look. Admittedly, I'm a game snob. However, I was in such deprivation, I didn't care what game it was—I *needed* to play something. Anything! My sanity was at stake.

I crossed the dirt parking lot and opened the door. A happy chime sounded, announcing my not-so-happy presence. Just before I stepped inside, I turned to take one last look over my shoulder. There weren't any monsters following me, but the storm was almost directly overhead.

I felt the first few droplets of rain spray me in the face.

I shuddered and went inside.

About the Authors

E.G. Foley is the pen name for a husband-and-wife writing team who live in Pennsylvania. They have been finishing each other's sentences since they were teens, so it was only a matter of time before they were writing together, too.

"E" is a 7-8th grade teacher of students who regularly use more than 10% of their brains, world traveler, ice cream connoisseur, and martial arts enthusiast. "G" loves big books and small fluffy creatures, and if she hadn't become a writer, would have pursued a career as either a princess or spy—or possibly both! With millions of copies of her adult novels from Random House and HarperCollins sold in sixteen languages around the world, she has been hitting bestseller lists regularly for the past decade.

You can visit them on the web at EGFoley.com and sign up for their newsletter to be notified when their next book is available.

Thanks for reading!

And for Fans of Fantasy and Magical Adventures, check out

The Gryphon Chronicles by E.G. Foley

"A wonderful novel in the same vein as Harry Potter, full of nonstop action, magical creatures, and the reality that was Queen Victoria's England." —The Reading Café

The Gryphon Chronicles, Book 1: THE LOST HEIR
#1 Bestselling Children's Ebook on Amazon.com!

Strange new talents...
Jake is a scrappy orphaned pickpocket living by his wits on the streets of Victorian London. Lately he's started seeing ghosts and can move solid objects with his mind! He has no idea why. Next thing he knows, a Sinister Gentleman and his minions come hunting him, and Jake is plunged headlong into a mysterious world of magic and deadly peril. A world that holds the secret of who he really is: the long-lost heir of an aristocratic family with magical powers!

But with treacherous enemies closing in, it will take all of his wily street instincts and the help of his friends—both human and magical—to solve the mystery of what happened to his parents and defeat the foes who never wanted the Lost Heir of Griffon to be found...

NY Times and *USA Today* bestselling author E.G. Foley presents *The Gryphon Chronicles,* a series of historical fantasy adventures (with a hint of steampunk!) that's as much fun for grownups as it is for kids.

Discover the Magic!